THE CURSE OF HABITABLE WORLDS

PREETISH AGRAWAL

Made with ♥ on the Notion Press Platform
www.notionpress.com

To my Parents, Pramil and Shobha Agrawal, who have been an anchor in my continued sustenance of finding purpose and meaning in this world!

To my Sisters, Priya and Arshiya Agrawal, who have understood the importance of keeping me near the ground, while preserving my wings!

To Vanshika and Nityanshi, who had the patience to read a bunch of blubbered ideas, and help me create something beautiful!

To Carl Sagan, finding 'COSMOS' was equivalent to finding faith! Thank you for inspiring multiple souls like me who understand so little about our universe. Hope I can also contribute to the betterment of this Pale Blue Dot!

Contents

Contents

Preface

Science and religion, past and future, truth and false, love and hate, happiness and sadness; everything stems from the same thing, and yearns to get dissolved in the same mess. Our incapability of realizing the interdependence of paradoxical contrasts in the world is the foremost reason for conflict in our society!

The Curse of Habitable Worlds attempts to tame these heavy ideas with drama, humour, science, and faith! It attemps to be at the intersection of all these paradoxical realities, perfectly balancing all the sides, ultimately hoping to fail at the same.

This story is about love, but not a classic girl meets boy; it is about science, but shys away from scientific jargons; it is about religion, but it tip-toes around mythology; and it is set in the future, but does not feature flying cars!

It is about life, which like a culmination of so many things, is not really about anything, other than experiencing. Welcome to the small world that I have created. Leave your pre-conceived notions at the bottom of this page, and just experience a simple story...

CHAPTER ONE

LIFELESS

The year was 2073, and the world had taken a dystopian tone. A young couple sat outside the fertility clinic, on a hard iron bench. Their fists clenched each other's hand as tightly as they possibly could, for all the nervousness in their bodies had been navigated to that closed fist. The clenched fist was accompanied by a charm bracelet in Mallory's hand, with figurines of six planets and moons attached to the bracelet. Her husband Ankur had his eyes set on the charm bracelet. As the couple waited for their test results, they saw hundreds of eyes amidst them, carrying the same hope to the fertility clinic that they were carrying with them that day. This was a common sight at the Bombay National Fertility Clinic, a government-run service that was made available in nearly every major city of India, after the National Fertility Act of 2069.

Having children and a family had gradually shifted from becoming a norm in India to the biggest luxury. For a country that was known worldwide for its familial values and culture, the gradual decline in fertility led to the loss of the very thing that had brought it success, a skilled and young workforce. Around the world, infertility had hit its peak around 2070, after which it had plateaued. Today in India, only one in forty women can bear a child, a number that is estimated to rise to one in sixty by the year 2130. This scenario is worse in western countries, with the numbers rising to one in seventy in many countries. This gives every couple sitting in the fertility clinic a probability of only two and a half percent to have a family. The human species had always been afraid that overpopulation would be the end of them; but they had never imagined, that underpopulation would be the actual curse.

"WE ARE DONE FOR TODAY – PLEASE COME BACK TOMORROW", said the nurse at the fertility clinic as she locked the door.

The crowd got up, frustrated and devastated, and exited the fertility clinic. Mallory and Ankur could not gather the strength to get up from their bench, and a small droplet of tear rolled down Mallory's eyes. Hiding their mutual pain, Mallory got up with a friction.

"Anuradha Aunty called again. Could you please let her know we don't have anything left to support her", Mallory shouted, to hide her sadness.

"She is also lonely and dependent on us, could we not cut her some slack?", said Ankur.

"Everybody is lonely and dependent on us. Is it our fault that infertility rose exponentially when we were growing up? Why is it our duty to support so many old family members, just because they could not have kids?", Mallory's frustration was rising.

"How can you say that, Mal? Especially today, right here? Yes, they could not have kids, and they have already paid the biggest price for a mistake they did not even commit! Our small monetary contributions act as an ointment to the pain they have gone through", said Ankur as he exited the room. A tear rolled down his cheek, as he had just gone from being hopeful, to sad, to devastated.

Mallory opened her phone and transferred INR 50,000 to 'Aunt Anuradha' from her contact list.

As Mallory and Ankur came back to their small house on the outskirts on Navi Mumbai, Mallory saw what her life had become. A small house with two rooms and concrete gray walls, with a small bed in the smaller room of the house. Ankur and Mallory had together decided to keep the bigger room for their future child, where a polished wooden crib lay in the center of a large room.

"Please get ready by 9 AM tomorrow", Ankur pleaded as he dismissed himself into a pile of books in his study.

"Some of us have work, you realize that right?" said Mallory in a condescending tone, "Not really sure if I can ask for another day off."

"You are amongst the last ten astronomers left in the country, with nobody to report to, and not one person expecting any miracles." said Ankur, immediately regretting his words. He rushed outside of his study and held a sobbing Mallory in his hands.

"Not even you?" asked Mallory while sobbing uncontrollably. "Do you also believe that science cannot save us?"

"I am sorry. We both are devastated after our day and are taking it out on each other. I know our chance will come tomorrow; I am positive about it. Let us give it one more shot, please! I also cannot go alone and get myself checked for fertility, would get a bit awkward with the OB-GYN don't you think?", Ankur said jokingly. Mallory got a small smile on her face as she saw Ankur, and the hope that he carried in his eyes.

Humans were becoming completely infertile by the year 2067, resulting in them being incapable of reproducing on their own. Then, a miracle drug was developed by Dr.

Shyam Srivastava, allowing people with specific fertility chromosomes, aged between the ages of twenty-five and twenty-seven, to take the drug and become capable of reproduction. However, the drug was extremely costly, and could only be produced in a limited quantity every year. Then, the government enacted the National Fertility Act of 2069, under which everyone could approach their local fertility clinics and get themselves tested. If found capable of bearing a child, the government would provide the drug free of cost.

Next morning, Mallory and Ankur, like hundreds of couples every day, began their travel again to the fertility clinic.

"We just need to be lucky enough to get the token Mal, I know our result will be positive!" said Ankur excited as they began their hour-long journey.

"From where do you get so much optimism, Ankur? As a man of science, aren't you pushed towards the logical case scenario. The probability of us having a kid is only two and a half percent. I want a child as much as you do; but me wanting something does not change the probability of it happening, does it? Moreover, the application of this probability is also dependent on our token number ever being called out", said Mallory.

"How many planets do you know that have life Mal?", Ankur asked softly.

"Only Earth"

"The charm bracelet that you wear in your hand every day, it has six planets and moons that had the highest possibility of having life, right? How many traces did we find of life?"

"None"

"As per estimations, the last stars would die out 120 trillion years from now, which would be followed by 10^{106} years of just black holes. Condensed, it's like the universe starting with one second of stars and then billions and billions of years of just darkness with black holes. Stars my love, are an immediate after effect of the big bang, a sliver of sunlight coming through a dark thick cardboard, a ray of hope in a world filled with darkness. You and me, we are here in that one bright second", said Ankur in a deep voice.

Mallory looked at Ankur with a bit of confusion, coupled with a lot of love –

"Also, as Carl Sagan had said"

"Wait wait", Mallory interjected. "First the heath death theory, then Carl Sagan. What is going on? You know I can't resist all this flirtatious science talk", Mallory said playfully.

"As Carl had said", said Ankur with an even deeper voice, "We are just like butterflies, who flutter for a day and think that it is forever."

"But what has this got to do with probabilities and understanding the logical chance of something happening?", Mallory was now actually confused.

"It has got to do with faith. If you calculate the probability of us being here, in the grand scheme of things, you will never reach a number that would convince you to do anything. Look at all the beauty around you, do you think the light will give in to the darkness so easily? All I am asking you to do my love, is believe. I strongly believe that wanting something, and believing that it can happen, does tip the scales of probability into your favor. When we reach the clinic and sit with our clenched fists today, along with hope, do you promise me that you will also have a bit of faith?", said Ankur emotionally.

Being the daughter of an astronomer, Mallory was taught from a very young age that reasoning is the biggest strength a person can have. Her path to atheism was not only paved by the lack of evidence of a creator of the universe, but also by the improbability of it. However, today, as she walked to the token counter, she closed her eyes for ten seconds before she received the token and sat back on that hard iron bench.

In our most desperate times, logic and reasoning can only take us so far. When every calculation in the universe convinces you to not believe, luck only favors those who find belief. Mallory did not believe in any god that she could pray to, but her clenched fist today had the token number 7 displayed on it.

"Token number 7, Mallory and Ankur Shah", announced the nurse on the microphone.

The seven heavens and the seven hells all came colliding down at one instant in Mallory's gut. *All it takes, is a little bit of faith*", Mallory whispered to herself as she and Ankur stepped into the clinic for their one chance at having a family.

CHAPTER TWO

THE CHARM BRACELET

The air conditioner grizzled on the top of the room, trying to fight the escalating heat in India. Below, Mallory lay on the bed, with her eyes wide open. The test results usually took three to five days to come in, which translated to three to five sleepless nights for the anxious couple. Ankur, sitting in his study, had engrossed himself completely in his research. Mallory's eyes were fixated on her charm bracelet, which doubled as a fidget mechanism in her anxious moments.

"Europa, Titan, Gliese 667Cc, Kepler 22B, Kepler 69C, Trappist 1E", Mallory continuously whispered to herself, while fidgeting across the miniature versions of the moons and exoplanets.

"Europa, Titan, Gliese, umm; what was it dad? Gliese what?", Mallory suddenly found herself as a thirteen-year-old, sitting with her father in her father's observatory. Repetition and lack of sleep are the perfect recipe to bring back some long-lost memories.

The night sky looked the same as it was fifteen years ago, when a little twelve year old Mallory had her weekly date night with her father and a Celektron 8000 telescope.

Mr. Dhruv Jain was amongst the top Indian astronomers of his time. Every Saturday night, he ensured that Mallory and he would sit in their observatory, navigate the telescope towards the vast universe, and talk about astronomy.

"Remind me again, how big is the universe, daddy?" asked the curious little Mallory.

"The observable universe is around 90 billion light years in diameter. In the observable universe, there are around a hundred billion galaxies, and each galaxy has around a hundred billion stars," described Dhruv.

"These numbers are too big to imagine dad," said Mallory, unhappy with the analogy.

"Mallory my child, imagine, at an average, there are approximately ten thousand stars in the observable universe for every grain of sand that is there on earth", exclaimed Dhruv, knowing his daughter enjoyed analogies more than numbers.

"But what was the name of this third moon in my bracelet, Gliese 677," Mallory fumbled.

"Gliese 667Cc", said Dhruv. "It's an exoplanet, 22 light years away from us, that orbits a red dwarf star."

"Is a red dwarf star better than our sun?", questioned Mallory.

"It's more stable, and lives longer. I mean our sun would also become a dwarf someday."

"But why just six possibilities dad? If there are more stars than grains of sand on Earth, how is it possible that we have seen no proof of extraterrestrial life? Isn't it possible that there would be trillions of planets that would support life? Where are all the aliens?"

"That my child, is the Fermi Paradox," Dhruv said as he saw the curiosity build in his daughter's mind.

"MAL, aren't you getting late for work?", asked Ankur shaking her back to the present world.

As Mallory was transported back, she hurriedly got up, running around the house to collect all her belongings.

"Please don't spend the entire day in your study Ankur, at least take a walk around the block at some point, okay?", said Mallory as she stuffed a book in her handbag.

"I am very close to a breakthrough Mal. I am not even going to move from my seat, till I figure this one out."

"Is that an indication for me that I should remember and send your lunch?"

"I don't think I will have time to eat Mal", said Ankur nervously, knowing a scolding was coming his way.

"Babe, I will send your lunch around 1:30. Do have it. See you after work, love you", said Mallory as she rushed out of the house.

"Love you too!!" said Ankur as he sat back on his desk, exhausted. A board hung on his left, with the words 'THE MENTAL CASTLE' clipped as the heading, and hundreds of sticky notes engaged in a war to find place on the board. Ankur, the son of a wealthy businessman, was astonished by the workings of the mind from a very young age. After receiving his doctorate at the early age of twenty, Ankur had received a grant of INR 2,50,00,000 by the Indian Mind Research Project, to research on the possibility of developing an 'eidetic memory'. Ankur always believed that the human mind could develop a system, which he referred to as the 'Mental Castle', that would allow the human brain to remember every little detail that the eyes have ever seen. Today, after spending the entire grant money, and investing ten years of his life; Ankur was still awaiting his little breakthrough. While the guilt of not picking up a paying job, when there was an immense scarcity of skilled young workforce in the country, did resurface periodically; Ankur's mission in his mind was very clear. Ankur understood that the way for humanity to progress is not just by depending on machines and computers that aid humans in their operations, *but by truly unlocking the hidden potential in our biology.*

"All it takes a little belief Ankur, a little belief," he whispered to himself as he surrendered himself back to his books.

CHAPTER THREE

THE GREAT FILTER

The Indian Astronomical Association (IAA) was the last surviving astronomy association in India. After the rise of infertility, the delicate balance between the dependent and independent population of the country was disrupted. The rising dependent population had become one of the highest sectors of government expenditure. With the fiscal deficit on the rise, the blunt of this hit, was borne by science.

"Where is Chandrakant?", Mallory enquired as she stepped into the office, "Could you please let him know I want to discuss something with him?"

"He has gone to meet Uncle. Things have been quite intense around here for the last couple of days", answered Vega.

"What does Uncle want now; and why didn't you go with Chandrakant? You know Uncle can't digest your chiseled looks", Mallory said humorously.

"I offered to go. My chiseled looks are the only thing that has gotten us so much funding till now from Uncle", Vega said playfully.

"Chiseled looks, coupled with crores of rupees that Uncle has earned over the last three decades because of the technology and information we have created and given to him. The least he can do is continue funding us."

"You know we are amongst the last surviving astronomy association in the world, right? For years, when the government and the people believed that we would find some instances of life in the solar system, or terraform mars, money was flowing into space exploration. The last spaceship on which I went to Mars was completely operated by a crew of two without any help from ground control. Think of the engineering marvel we had achieved. But all this has now become dust Mallory. Don't you think we should accept this?", Vega said in a comforting tone.

"No, that is what the problem is. I understand we failed in creating an impact with space exploration, but that does not mean the endeavor has lost its value. If we fail an exam and quit, it speaks more about us than the exam itself. We destroyed Earth, and only humanity is to be blamed for it. But if we could not terraform Mars, that does not mean it is the end of astronomy. Government aid is only a short-term answer to our problems; someone will have to fund the search for new habitable worlds", said Mallory beaming with passion.

"Are there other worlds out there that we can reach? Worlds that have or can support life? How many of our initial guesses have been correct about planets with life?", inquired Chandrakant.

"YOU TOO? DOES NOBODY ELSE BELIEVE IN OUR WORK ANYMORE EXCEPT ME?", shouted Mallory, unable to contain her emotions.

"No Mallory.", Chandrakant replied calmly.

"Uncle has pulled our funding. He called me today not to lecture about the lack of results that our research has brought in, but to ask one simple question. The amount of money that has been flowing into this facility, why should it not flow for medical research, or food research, or anything else tangible, that can help in betterment of people's lives? I could not answer him. We lost", said Chandrakant, with tears rolling down his eyes.

Mallory's anger dissolved into dismay, as she sat down on the floor. The initial denial that had set in after the life-changing news was slowly fading, giving way to desolation. An eerie silence surrounded the room.

"Where did we go wrong Chandrakant? Why did we fail?"

"Astronomy, more than any other field of science out there, relies on people's imagination and hope. To fund our research and our space faring missions, people need to believe that they belong amongst the stars. We did not lose Mallory; the hope lost. We are just paying the price of its loss", said Chandrakant as the entire room looked at him in silence.

"We have until the end of day today to clear everything out. Thank you for all the work, guys. Drinks are on me at the day's end", said Chandrakant as he excused himself to his cabin.

A devastated Mallory was sitting at her desk, when everyone around her were finishing their last assignment.

"THE GREAT FILTER MIGHT BE THE ONLY ANSWER TO THE FERMI PARADOX", were the words written on a sticky note on Mallory's desk.

"That my child, is the Fermi Paradox", the words of her father discovered their way back to Mallory's mind as she went back to the memory lane.

Dhruv had an immense capacity to simplify complicated scientific concepts for little Mallory.

"What you have asked me kiddo, was also asked by the noble laureate Enrico Fermi in 1950, which gives rise to the 'Fermi Paradox'. Reflecting on the vastness of the cosmos, Fermi had asked – 'Where are they?', referring to extraterrestrials and life beyond earth. While we have had several great minds researching this proposition, we haven't found even one concrete answer. Even our own galaxy, the Milky Way, has around four hundred billion stars. Think of all the life that would be teeming out there in the heat of these stars.", said Dhruv as he saw the curiosity light up inside little Mallory.

"Is space travel so hard, that none of these life forms could have figured out how to come to Earth?", said Mallory as she looked up at the night sky.

"Sounds unlikely right?", said Dhruv.

"But there must be an answer" Mallory was now getting restless with all the probabilities.

"Answer, no, but I do have a hypothesis, which is called the great filter" said Dhruv as he saw the eyes of his little daughter lit up.

"The great filter is the utmost important inflection point and the most improbable step, that a civilization needs to cross to decide the origination and continuity of life. Either, the filter can be abiogenesis, the arising of life out of lifelessness; or, it can be the continuity of life, growing into intelligent multicellular species like us, and then being able to survive long enough to wake up from our technological adolescence" Dhruv explained, afraid that he had made the simple question too complex.

"But wait, this doesn't make sense" Mallory interjected. "By your example, the great filter can either be behind us or ahead of us. How does this help our understanding? Your hypothesis gives us no answers whatsoever." Mallory exclaimed.

"Well, my dear, *some hypotheses are not made to give us answers, but to help us ask better questions!* The charm bracelet I gave you has six possibilities, maybe you can create one that has hundreds of them", said Dhruv, impressed by how quickly Mallory had digested the information and reached a logical question.

"MALLORY! YOU NEED TO SEE THIS. MALLORY", shouted Vega trying to bring Mallory back to the present.

"We have found something, you need to see this", Vega rushed her to get up from her desk.

"What can be important now Vega, even I have lost the will."

"Oumuamua", said Vega as he saw Mallory astounded by the word.

CHAPTER FOUR

OUMUAMUA

Oumuamua was the first interstellar object that visited our solar system back in 2017. It was a rocky, cigar shaped object, that was around four hundred meters in length. While initially believed to be a comet, large telescopes could detect that the object was an interstellar object. Observations had suggested that it had been wandering through the Milky Way, unattached to any star system for hundreds of millions of years, before its chance encounter with our star system.

"Are you sure its Oumuamua? For nearly a century, no other interstellar object was sighted by any observatory around the world. When did it last visit us, 2017?", said Mallory.

"Yes, the kid found it", said Vega, pointing to a man who looked like he was in his thirties.

"Kid? How is he a kid Vega? Scratch that, who are you?", said Mallory confused, as she had never seen the man before at the observatory.

"Hi Mallory, I am Vayu Srivastava. I am an intern with the team, and I joined yesterday. It is my good fortune to be working with you", said Vayu extending his hand to introduce himself to Mallory.

"An intern? Aren't you a little old to be an intern? Also, did you not hear the announcement in the morning? There is no working with us anymore", said Mallory in a condescending tone.

"What is with all the hostility Mallory? The kid did a great job. None of us could identify that one of the twin comets was the Oumuamua, that too so quickly", said Vega supporting Vayu.

"Scientific endeavor is not one of speed Vega, but of precision. How do you know its Oumuamua?", questioned Mallory.

"It was bright by around a factor of ten than any other comet, and it spun on its axis approximately every seven hours. Its unique shape is not found in any comet of our solar system", answered Vayu diligently.

"How is this possible? Rohan, pull up the trajectory data of Oumuamua from 2017. It should have never appeared again in the night sky basis the trajectory that it was originally on.", said Mallory as she analyzed the data Vayu had referred to.

"Twin, did you say a twin comet Vega?", Mallory stopped suddenly as she was waiting for the facts to sink in.

"Yes, it's the weirdest thing. I did not even know the same was possible", said Vega.

"Who found it, can one of you show me?"

"The kid did", said Vega, pointing to Vayu who was slowly getting a smirk on his face.

"Wipe off that smirk and show me what you saw. You must have seen a twin tailed comet. You know that it is not possible for comets to come so close to each other and survive, right?" said Mallory as she got irritated with the presence of Vayu in her observatory.

"It's not a twin tailed comet. It's something that we saw yesterday and believed to be two comets flying very close to each other and somehow surviving. Today, we realized that one of them is Oumuamua", explained Vayu.

"Did you calculate the trajectory path of the second one?", asked Mallory.

"We were running the numbers when the announcement came in this morning. It is a little far, won't be able to calculate with much certainty. Not in a day's time", expressed Vega.

"I can help fasten up the process", said Vayu as he diligently started crunching codes on the desktop.

"Who the hell is he? And why is he here suddenly on our last day?"

"Limit the hostility, Mallory. He is just someone who is immensely interested, but we could afford another hire, so he offered to help for free."

"But don't you think we would have noticed these comets; don't we keep track of these things? How did this comet anomaly happen the day the kid stepped in?", said Mallory with concern.

"Maybe he is doing a few things better than all of us. That is the only answer I can think of", said Vega.

"MALLORY! MALLORY! MALLORY!", Vayu started shouting.

"Relax. What happened?!!".

"You need to see this, we need to get this confirmed by someone else", said Vayu pointing towards the screen.

"PROBABILITY OF IMPACT WITH EARTH – EIGHT PERCENT", showcased on the screen.

"What the hell?" Mallory pushed Vayu's chair away from the desktop as she hurriedly pulled another one and started crunching numbers on the desktop. Vega ran in the background to get Chandrakant from his cabin.

"Chandrakant, are you seeing this? Twin comet, one weirdly Oumuamua, and the other, on a direct trajectory to collide with Earth", said Mallory pointing towards her screen.

"Relax Mallory, take a breath. Probability of impact is eight percent, correct?"

"Yes", nodded Mallory in shock.

"Rohan, pull up data to check if there are remnants of any dart missions from the last century that are still functioning", Chandrakant ordered.

"Calculate the time of impact."

"If it maintains its trajectory, eighty-eight days from now", answered Mallory.

"No dart mission remnants found", said Rohan.

"Fastest dart mission in history?"

"A little south of a year", answered Vayu as the room fell completely silent.

Chandrakant got up and went back to his cabin. Dart mission meant the 'Double Asteroid Redirection Test', that was carried out to change the trajectory of a near earth object by colliding the object with a small spaceship, thus stopping it from impacting Earth.

"Do you think we can prevent it in eighty-eight days?", asked Vayu.

"No. Three hundred days was achieved by NASA when their space research and development was working at its best capacity. We don't have the personnel, nor the funds to pull off anything like that, especially in eighty-eight days. Have we finally reached the great filter?" said Mallory with an immense dismay on her face.

"Our SOS has been cancelled", said Chandrakant reemerging from the background.

"What? How can anybody cancel the SOS? The world needs to know about this", said Mallory furiously.

"There is no space agency left in the world Mallory. There is nobody willing to fund this, and honestly, do you think we can even pull off something like this?", asked Chandrakant.

"But with an impact Chandrakant, the world could potentially end. Don't you realize that?"

"There is an eight percent chance of impact. There is a ninety two percent chance that nothing happens. The odds are not in our favor", said Chandrakant.

"Talk to Uncle, I am sure he will understand."

"Uncle is the one who cancelled the SOS Mallory. He is still pulling off funding on an immediate basis. He believes this information can only cause distress and panic in an already rotting world, with no real-world solutions available", said Chandrakant.

"So, I guess there won't be a hero moment for us then? The moment where the world comes together after an extreme adversity and pull off something that is impossible?", said Vega.

"No Vega, we are not even allowed to attempt our hero moment. This is privately funded research, so if a word of this gets out, all our necks are on the line", warned Chandrakant.

"Hold on a second, so what are we supposed to do exactly? Nothing?" Mallory was frustrated beyond her core.

"Pray. Pray to everything you believe in, that we don't fall within the outcome of eight percent", said Chandrakant as he left the observatory.

"THIS IS THE MOST RIDICULOUS THING I HAVE HEARD IN MY LIFE", shouted Mallory as she exited the observatory.

"If the world was ending in a few days, as a common man living his life, do you think you would want to know", Vayu asked Vega softly.

"I would. *But it should be presented to me in a way I could digest. Otherwise, it's total chaos*", Vega answered as he left the room.

CHAPTER FIVE

MENTAL CASTLE

While Mallory was yelling furiously at whoever she could find in the observatory, Ankur had submitted himself to the realm of his study. After several sleepless nights, Ankur had entered a mental state where he was unable to grasp the present. This state took him back to his most impactful memory.

A young twelve-year-old boy sat at the footsteps of the Rajaji palace in Jaipur, one of the last existing monarchial palaces in the world. With seven inhabitants and one hundred staff members to maintain the lavish 110 acres palace, Rajaji palace was a sight to behold. Rajaji shah, the king of the palace, while having no practical bureaucratic or political powers, had immense control over the matters of the country. He made this possible by holding valuable secrets of the most influential people that ran the nation.

Rajaji's son, Ankur Shah, was the sole inheritor of all the riches and power that the Rajaji palace had to offer. Being a very bright kid, Ankur had an immense capacity to exercise his mind, remember mundane patterns, and solve exceptional analytical problems.

"One day you will inherit everything that you see around you. Excited?!", asked Rajaji looking at his twelve-year-old son.

"Excited is a strong word. I don't really care about the riches dad", said Ankur in a mature tone.

"Nor should you", Ankur's mother entered from behind. "Out of everything that is here in this palace, which object is the most valuable, Ankur?"

"The palace itself I suppose", said Ankur.

"Wrong. Even more than the palace, the small safe in your dad's study, the one no is allowed to go near to", hinted his mother.

"Why? What is there? Diamonds?"

"No, my son, more valuable than diamonds! Information", said Rajaji. "Always in life, try to control the flow of information, and you will witness yourself controlling everything and everyone around you. One day, when you inherit all this, you will inherit the information in that safe".

"INFORMATION, always INFORMATION", Ankur was trembling as the past was coming to haunt him back.

The next time Ankur saw the safe, his parents were held at gunpoint by five dacoits, threatening to cross any line to attain the information in the safe. The royal textured Rajaji Palace turned gloomy in an instant in Ankur's mind. They had first shot his mother, then his two uncles and two aunts. Rajaji stood there, not uttering a single word. He knew, no matter what, the dacoits will kill everyone in the room. The people living in the palace were so influential, that letting anybody live was equivalent to signing a death sentence for the dacoits.

"The boy cannot hurt you, he is a child", Rajaji begged the dacoits as they pointed the gun at Ankur's face. "I know you will kill me no matter what, I have made my peace with it. Please let me save my child."

"Just give the combination of the safe, or I am pulling the trigger", a dacoit said.

"Wait! What if I donate the Rajaji Palace to the citizens of Jaipur. Let the government transform it into a hotel and the proceeds go into the development of the city. I will strip my child of his title and inheritance. With no influence, you should have no reason to kill him, right?", said Rajaji.

"Are the palace's papers in the safe as well?", said one of the dacoits.

"Yes"

Ankur remembered as a child, the horror of seeing the blood of all his family members painting the Rajaji Palace in its last glory. He was soon shifted out of the property and was kept in trauma custody for six months. During these months, Ankur would get nightmares of the murders at the palace and would wake up shouting things with immense details. He would often talk about the small visible scar on the hand of one of the dacoit that shot his mother, and the crippling foot of another who had opened the safe. While the faces of all the dacoits were covered, the horror in Ankur's nightmares allowed him to see every detail that happened that night. Anuradha Kashyap, a doctor in the facility noticed this miracle in memory, that trauma had allowed Ankur to possess. His greatest gift was also his biggest nightmare.

"Aunt Anuradha, I want to go talk to the police", said little Ankur.

"Ankur, we talked about this; the dacoits ensured that they exited with hundreds of staff from the palace, there is no way of figuring out who they actually were. More than half of the house help at the palace was always recruited on a day-to-day basis. There is nothing the police can do", said Anuradha to comfort the grieving child.

"I will recognize them. I can remember distinct details about all of them", said Ankur.

"But how can the police believe you kid? Weren't they all wearing masks. There is no way your testimony would be submitted as adequate evidence."

Over the next six nights, Ankur, during his nightmares, focused on the combination of the safe that his dad had conveyed to the dacoits. The safe had a twenty-four number combination, the probability of guessing which was close to zero. After six nights, Ankur went to the police station, demonstrated to the police that if he could remember the combination to the safe, he could recognize the mannerisms of the dacoits.

"Prodigy child brings his murdered family to justice; remembers specific details from his dreams", read an elaborate article that was published about Ankur in the national newspapers.

Ankur had become an overnight sensation, with multiple colleges offering scholarships for him to attend. At a tender age, Ankur became obsessed with the workings of the mind, the one weapon that supported him when nothing else did.

Today, with the Mental Castle, Ankur is trying to bridge this gap we have between our dreams and reality, between the conscious and the subconscious. *Everything that we perceive is stored in our subconscious mind in some capacity.* With dreams, we can find a way of getting into this transient state, where we could access the subconscious for all the required information. Once this is perfected, man would figure out how to obtain an 'eidetic memory'. The problem is that this bridge is only formulated for events that shake the entire core of our existence. Life changing alterations, mostly negative events that torment us.

Over the last ten years, Ankur has been constantly practicing his ability to channelize the Mental Castle, even for the good memories.

"Imagine, if I would never forget the birth of my child, or its first walk. If all its happy memories could clog my Mental Castle, maybe the nightmare of the Rajaji Palace would become a background noise", he whispered to himself.

While Ankur had been constantly increasing his capacity, he knew that there was a long road ahead of him.

CHAPTER SIX

FERTILITY

An unopened box of mac and cheese lay on the dining table, a broken wooden crib stood in the middle of a large room, and an eerie silence filled Mallory and Ankur's house. Beside the crib, sat Ankur, hopelessly trying to mend what he had destroyed. In the other room, lay Mallory. Her tears had drained every ounce of hydration left in her body.

"Don't fixate on the crib Ankur, you will hurt yourself", said Mallory from across the room.

"Not more than me being fixated on you has hurt me", Ankur said in an insensitive tone.

"I don't have the energy to do this anymore, Ankur. Can we please have a civilized conversation?"

"So, you do know what civilized means. Congratulations!"

"It's not our fault, things are not in our control, let us not be so insensitive towards each other. Please", said Mallory as she got up and walked towards the crib. "We will get a new one, don't worry."

"It's not the crib I am worried about Mal, it's us."

"There is nothing to worry about, everything is fine. We are just drained. You also did not have the lunch I sent you. Should I heat it up?"

"I don't think I would be able to swallow."

"You will if I feed you from my own hands. Come, I am waiting for you at the dining table", said Mallory as she got up to heat the mac and cheese.

'BOMBAY NATIONAL FERTILITY CLINIC', read an opened envelope that laid on the table beside the food. Mallory shrugged the envelope away, picked up the food and strode towards the kitchen to heat it up.

"So how was your day? Did you get the breakthrough you were talking about in the morning?", Mallory said from across the kitchen to keep the chain of conversation open.

"Ankur, will you answer me please?", said Mallory as she walked out of the kitchen and saw Ankur reading the envelope on the dining table.

"Why are you torturing yourself?", said Mallory as she picked up the food and sat on the dining table.

"Tell me about your day. Any new breakthroughs? Anything interesting?", said Mallory as she removed the envelope from Ankur's hands, and fed him the first bite.

"Major breakthrough. I concluded today that my wife is a bitch", said Ankur as he gulped down the bite.

Mallory stared at Ankur with a dead serious look, then they both broke into laughter.

"If I am a bitch, what does that make you?", said Mallory as she hugged Ankur tightly.

"Are you sure about this Mal? Please think about it again"

"Let us not get started again. Give it a rest please. I told you what happened today right", said Mallory as she fed him another bite.

"But look at this", Ankur reached again for the envelope and opened it.

'It gives us immense pleasure to inform you that you have successfully passed the fertility test. However, we also wish to caution you that your fertility has been met in grade 3. We have sent across the fertility pill along with this envelope, and we advise you to be instantaneous in your consumption of it', read the envelope.

"Are you sure about your decision. Delay in taking the pill by three months could immensely hurt our chances of conceiving."

"Did you not hear when I told you what happened today?", asked Mallory as she got up from the dining table.

"There is a possibility that the world is going to end. How can you think about bringing a life to this world at this point in time?"

"Because that is all I have thought about for the last two years as we have visited the fertility clinic, when we bought this wooden crib, and when we polished it every night after our token number was not called out", said Ankur.

"*If we give a life, is it our right to take it*? I want this as much as you do my love, but I cannot do it. How can I, in good conscience, conceive my child in a world that is coming to an end. If we decide to go ahead with this, isn't it equivalent to taking the life of our own child? How do you not see this?", said Mallory as she came and sat back on the table.

"All I see is an extremely paranoid scientist. All I see is a person who gets rattled by events so instantly, that she has no resolve or commitment left within herself, or with her partner. I was ready to accept if fate and biology would have robbed us of a chance of having a family; But I never thought the one to commit the heist would be you Mal", said Ankur as he refused to take in another bite from Mallory's hands.

"The thing that I see is a gross overreaction. A world ending event is approaching at our door in less than three months, and you want to bring in another life to the planet to get engulfed with it! If we are lucky enough that the comet does not burn us to our core, the world will still be here, so will the pill. I can take the pill after the probable date of impact crosses", said Mallory as she gulped down the bite herself that Ankur had refused.

"But that would decrease our probability of conceiving. The envelope says that instantaneous consumption is recommended", said Ankur.

"Now that is very convenient, isn't it. When I mention probabilities, when I argue with logic, you bring in faith and emotion. But now, our probabilities are declining if we wait a few months", said Mallory with a sarcastic tone.

Ankur took a long breath, came closer to Mallory and held her hands.

"Tell me Mal. If we delay this for three more months. If the world falls in the lucky ninety two percent and the comet goes past dwindling in the night sky. If we take the pill and are still unable to conceive. Would you be able to forgive yourself? Would you not blame yourself for not doing everything that you could to have our family?".

"Tell me Ankur. If we take the pill today and conceive. If we find out that we are having our child. If the world falls in the unlucky eight percent and the comet comes and impacts the Earth's surface. When the comet approaches, will you be able to forgive yourself? Will you not blame yourself for knowingly bringing a life into this world that could get obliterated?"

"I guess you will always be a pessimist. Just take the pill. We will not conceive till your eight percent chance comet goes dwindling through the sky", Ankur requested.

"If you force me today to take the pill, what will not stop you from forcing us tomorrow to conceive. I don't even recognize you anymore", said Mallory as she got up from the table and went back to the bedroom.

"She doesn't recognize me...", Ankur started murmuring to himself. "This is what she does, always. Will get paranoid over an event, take stupid decisions, and then regret over it later and cry. She might forgive herself for hurting our chances, but I won't be able to. Everything will be fine tomorrow morning. She would understand in a few weeks", murmured Ankur as he got up from the table.

The melancholic night in the Shah residence had passed. Ankur was sleeping on the bed, a deep sleep that had greeted him after days of insomnia. Mallory laid beside Ankur, fidgeting with her charm bracelet. She no longer recognized the man who was her husband. She got up, had a glass of water that lay on her bedside table, and went into Ankur's study.

'I am going away for a few days. Where? I don't know. I just need to leave. I can't do this anymore', wrote Mallory on a piece of paper as she stuck the paper on the board. She picked up a bag, threw in a few clothes, and left the house.

The empty glass of water that she had left on her bedside table had small, powdered remains of the medicine that was fused with the water. The envelope from the fertility clinic laid in the dustbin, along with an empty packet of the fertility pill. As Ankur enjoyed the deep sleep laying alone in his bed, Mallory walked the streets of Mumbai, clueless about the reason for Ankur's rem sleep.

CHAPTER SEVEN

OBSERVATORY

Mallory sat on the sidewalk, as she saw the IAA being torn down and stripped of its parts. With a bag in hand, and nowhere to go, Mallory for the first time in her life felt homeless. The observatory in the association used to be her solace, the place where she would come when she wanted to run away from the world. Today, as the world was racing past her, she was witnessing the last hope of humanity dying.

"It's like the last hope of humanity dying, isn't it?", said a voice from behind.

Mallory, astonished as if someone had read her thoughts, turned behind in excitement. Her excitement slowly faded to glee once she saw the source of the voice.

"Why are you here? What do you want?", asked Mallory in disgust.

"Why do you hate me? What have I ever done to you?", asked a familiar voice.

"I am sorry, Vayu. It is unfair of me to treat you this way. It's just that you were the only new thing that was there in what can be said to be the worst moment of my life, and I subconsciously started blaming you for everything.", said Mallory apologetically.

"I understand. What was the worst moment though? Knowing that there is a possibility that the world might end, or getting to know that the observatory was being shut down?", asked Vayu.

"If I can be selfish, it was losing the observatory. IAA was not just one of the places where we could engage in scientific endeavor, it was also my place of peace. Ever since I was a kid, sitting in my father's observatory, beneath the stars, is where I really felt that I am home", confessed Mallory.

"Where did your dad work?"

"He was the head astronomer of SOCO"

"What did they use back then? Was it Celektron?"

"Yes, the Celektron 8000", said Mallory, impressed with Vayu's knowledge of telescopes.

"I think I can help you here. Come with me", said Vayu as he extended his hand towards Mallory.

"I don't even know you. What if you kidnap me?"

"Considering how the last few days have been, would being kidnapped by a stranger really be the worst thing?"

Mallory considered for a moment, then took Vayu's hand as they walked to a car parked nearby.

"You drive a Jaguar? Are you rich Vayu?"

"Don't worry. It was a gift."

"Why would I be worried. I would have chosen an alto over the sidewalk. The jaguar feels like a lottery."

"Don't overuse the word lottery, you have a lot to see today", said Vayu as they drove away.

While Mallory was exploring new things with a new friend, Ankur had just woken up back in their residence. With several sleepless nights, a mentally draining conversation, and some actions that Ankur faintly remembered, he was walking across the house like a zombie.

"MAL! MAL!", he shouted as he did not find a trace of anyone in the house. As Ankur stumbled upon the note, the last three days came back to him in a second, and he sat back on the floor. With disdain over what he had done, Ankur knew he needed to go out and apologize to Mallory.

The wheels of jaguar halted in front of a huge gate, that scanned Vayu's eyes before they opened apart.

"Welcome to my humble aboard", said Vayu with a smirk on his face.

"That smirk, oh man it drives me crazy", said Mallory with a smile. "You know there is nothing humble about your entire existence, right?".

"Why do you judge so hastily? Give my existence some time. You never know what might surprise you", said Vayu winking at Mallory.

"Oh mister. There are no surprises happening here. I am a happily married woman. Let me warn you if we have gotten off on the wrong foot", said Mallory defensively.

"Haha, I did not mean it like that Mal. I was just referring to a surprise that I think you would really enjoy", said Vayu laughing.

"It's Mallory, not Mal. Nobody is allowed to call me Mal", said Mallory as she was getting more defensive of the overfriendly stranger.

"I am sorry. I just thought Mal suited better", said Vayu as he drove towards the backside of the house.

"Does the front gate not work? Why are we going in towards the back?"

"Because as much as you think I am interested in you madam, I am not trying to take you to my room."

Mallory sat in the car confused. As Vayu drove to the back of his house, Mallory saw something that resembled an observatory. All her guards were lowered in an instant.

"Is that an observatory Vayu?"

"I will do you one better. It's an observatory with a Celektron 8000 that my dad bought from SOCO. The jaguar does not seem so impressive now, does it?"

"It equates to an Alto now", said Mallory as she jumped off the car and ran towards the observatory.

CHAPTER EIGHT

FRIEND

Vayu's observatory had a new visitor, or what we could call, an old friend. Being alone in that observatory took Mallory back to the days when she craved date nights with her dad. Since her arrival, Vayu had been a complete gentleman. After showing her around the observatory, he had gone back to his bungalow, and had not disturbed Mallory till the next morning. The disturbance next morning came in the form of a breakfast platter.

"Who are you?", asked Mallory.

"Have you ever heard of Dr. Shyam Srivastava?"

"Shit! You are the son of Dr. Shyam Srivastava, the creator of the-"

"Fertility pill. Yes. But did you know his real interest was always astronomy?", said Vayu.

"Really? I never knew he studied astronomy."

"He did not. In his time, with infertility on the rise, nearly every scientist on the planet was forced to study biology. People knew that if something resembling the fertility pill had not been developed, it would have been the end of humanity", said Vayu.

"Yet here we are, facing another end of the world event. What do you think your dad would do if he was here?", asked Mallory.

"Get the best minds in the world together, give them whatever resources we have, and find a solution."

"Do you think a solution is possible?"

"I don't really know. The Celektron 8000 is very old technology, and I don't think we can measure the comet's trajectory. Not now. But I think we can get a fair estimate once the comet gets a bit closer", said Vayu.

"But what good would that do? Wont that be very late for any practical solutions?"

"At the least, we would know before the non-science believers, when the world is coming to an end. What would you do if you had that information?"

"Nothing. *If there is really no hope for anything to be done, I would rather be oblivious than omniscient*", said Mallory.

"So, you would rather be a nobody, than be a God?"

"What?", said Mallory as she looked at Vayu with disbelief.

"Isn't God, omniscient? Isn't he supposed to be the one who knows everything?", asked Vayu.

"Nobody knows everything. To think that you do, is the primal example of being a mortal"

Vayu saw the expression on Mallory's face changing from one of gratitude to disgust.

"Anyway, I need to go run some errands. Have kept food for you in the downstairs fridge. Will be back in an hour", said Vayu as he was leaving the observatory.

"Vayu why are you being so nice to me?", asked Mallory.

"Your dad had been a great inspiration for me growing up. You reek of his presence. Would love to know about him, maybe at night? Under the stars, with a glass of wine in hand?", asked Vayu.

"Sure", whispered Mallory, and her expression was enough for Vayu to understand.

Mallory spent the entire day in the observatory, combating her thoughts.

"Ankur must be worried about me. I shouldn't have left the way I did. He was just devastated", Mallory thought to herself.

As Mallory placed a call to Ankur, she did not know what she was going to say. She just knew that she needed to hear from him.

"Where are you MAL, I have been worried sick", said Ankur on the phone.

"Hi. I am okay. I came to a friend's house, he has an observatory in the back of his house", said Mallory.

"Are you still looking at the comet? Are you still fixated on that bloody improbable mess?", Ankur said angrily.

"What do you mean, Ankur? Do you really think, like other people, that we are just overreacting", asked Mallory.

"Yes Mallory. When in hell would you learn to grow up? You are one of those stupid children, who have been told fairy tales about their life in the stars by their fathers; and they could never step out of that fairy tale into the real world. There is nothing you can do to save the world, Mal. Neither from the comet, nor from the abomination this world has become. Astronomy, like you Mallory Shah, has become obsolete. Please get up from the freaking observatory, enter the real world, and come back home. I can't take this anymore.", Ankur exploded on the phone.

"Do you think everything my dad had said to me was just a fairy tale?", asked a sobbing Mallory.

A peculiar silence filled the conversation. Suddenly, a disconnecting tone played on the phone, and the phone fell from Mallory's hand on the floor and shattered into pieces.

CHAPTER NINE

BOUGHT CHILDREN

As Vayu entered the observatory, he saw Mallory, sitting on the floor, crying. Vayu rushed towards Mallory, with a glass of water in his hand,

"What happened Mal", he asked, as Mallory looked at him with rage. "Mal-lory, I was completing the name, give me a minute. It feels like you will detonate me with that rage, that too for calling half a name", Vayu said jokingly.

"The last few weeks, for the lack of a better word, have been exhausting beyond my core", said Mallory.

"I think you need to just unwind yourself a bit. When things get so difficult, I think it helps to gain perspective of why we loved some things in the first place. Tell me, what made you fall in love with astronomy?", asked Vayu, as he poured her a glass of wine.

"The sheer size of it. Growing up, I was always haunted by my purpose in this world. Dad always used to be busy with work, and I did not have a mom. There was no spirituality in our household. I just never understood what humanity was doing on this planet, and where we were supposed to go from here. When I was first told about the size of the observable universe, I could not even wrap my head around it. Why are we created so small when the universe is so big. Why does Einstein's law of special relativity place an insurmountable limit on our speed of travel and does not allow us to travel faster than the speed of light. From a very young age, I felt this innate aggression that there was so much out there, and that no matter how hard we try, we cannot explore even a tiny percent of it.", said Mallory with moist eyes as she gulped down the glass of wine.

"That is why it is so important for you that astronomy survives. You cannot comprehend a world where we have lost our spirit of exploration, can you?", asked Vayu.

"I can comprehend that world; I just don't feel like being a part of it."

"Me neither", said Vayu as he poured Mallory another glass of wine.

"Did your mother pass away, or were you a bought child as well?", asked Vayu

"As well! I understand that you were a bought child.", said Mallory.

"Yes, I was. My father's wife could not pass the fertility test herself, and dad wanted to continue working on the medicine. He experimented a different dose on her, and she died due to a complication from the medicine", said Vayu.

"It was after her death that your dad stopped his research?"

"Yes. He blamed his research for her death. This made conceiving strictly possible only for those who could pass the test."

"When did he buy you?", Mallory questioned.

"Around thirty-three years ago. I believe I was amongst the first ones to get adopted by the purchase route", Vayu exclaimed.

"Do you support this? Buying children from their biological parents for money?", asked Mallory.

"I do. For a long time, the world was stagnant in its technological prowess. This allowed certain social practices to settle in our society. But as times change, so will our social practices. My dad provided me with a good life, I am sure your dad did too! I am nothing but grateful", said Vayu as he laid down on the observatory.

"Do you know what Mallory means Vayu?"

"No"

"It means unfortunate. My dad believed that his was the last generation that had a world which was easy to live in. He knew anybody who came after them, had a tough task ahead of them. While his mind conjectured that having me was the wrong thing to do, his heart could not concur. He hence bought me with that pinch of salt in his head.", said Mallory.

"He wasn't completely wrong, was he? Our generation, we are at an inflection point. We are a bit unfortunate if you think about it", said Vayu as he consoled Mallory.

"Anyway, what about you? What made you fall in love with astronomy?", asked Mallory.

"For me, it was the precision of it. Have you ever looked at the sky and wondered, why is the size of the moon and the sun same in our night sky?", said Vayu as he pointed to the shiny moon in the sky. "The moon is $1/400^{th}$ the size of the sun; and $1/400^{th}$ the distance from the Earth, when compared to that of the sun. Do you realize that out of thousands of exoplanets that we have discovered till date, no other planet has been observed to have this coincidence.", said Vayu as Mallory looked at his face in awe.

"If the force of gravity was even a tiny bit stronger...", Vayu continued, "we would have all crumbled into a ball, and life would not have originated. If it was even a tiny bit weaker, the star systems would not have emerged, and we would have been starless and lifeless. *We look at the world around us and think we are the makers of it; but we are just its benefactors, that too not a respectable one.* There is an immense precision in the clockwork of the universe that has made this moment possible Mallory. Only if we had learnt to respect it earlier, we would not have driven ourselves into this disarray", said Vayu, with a seriousness in his face and hope in his twinkling eyes.

"If you are so in awe with the precision, do you also believe that there is a creator out there?", said Mallory.

"I cannot completely overlook that possibility. I don't know if there is a creator. I also don't know if the multiverse theory is correct?"

"I do not think that the multiverse theory is related to ay of this?", accused Mallory.

"Put simply, the multiverse theory states that it might be possible that there are several universes out there. There are a few physical constants in our universe, like the force of gravity or the speed of light, that have a specific assigned value that does not change. Out of all the universes out there, our universe is lucky enough to have the perfect combination of physical constants, allowing us to have a chance at this miracle", said Vayu as he held Mallory's hand.

"But that does not negate the possibility of a creator, does it?", asked Mallory.

"The onus is not on me to negate anything. As beings who have discovered so less about things are so close to us, we can just develop theories and believe what our faith allows us to believe", said Vayu, getting closer to Mallory.

"That is fascinating. *So, you don't need to really believe that there is a creator so be grateful for the universe?*", asked Mallory.

"I think for people in general, it is much easier to believe that someone made all this happen than to think that all of this is just an event of chance."

"Vayu, what do you exactly believe in?"

"I believe we can have any belief, as long as it helps us respect the intricacy of our existence. If we achieve that, I believe that if given a chance to do it again, humanity could handle things in a much better manner", said Vayu as he looked deep into Mallory's eyes.

"Vayu is this what faith feels like?", said Mallory softly as she started kissing Vayu passionately.

CHAPTER TEN

DECODED

On the other side of the city, in their residence at Navi Mumbai, a half angry and half ashamed, dreamy Ankur rushed to his study trying to find a charger for his phone. Since his call with Mallory had gotten disconnected due to battery drainage, Ankur was sitting in his study, repenting every word that he had said. Mallory's phone was unreachable, and none of her friends knew where she was.

"Who can be the friend with a freaking observatory?", wondered Ankur.

The call was continuously playing in Ankur's head, rewinding like a cassette tape.

"Do I remember the conversation with too much precision?", Ankur said to himself, as he sat on his chair. Suddenly, something astonishing happened. Ankur could remember everything from the phone call, even the background noise and the static disturbance that he had been experiencing recently on his calls. In Ankur's head, the exact static disturbance, that occurred on his phone calls, started playing.

"I need to do something about this", said Ankur as he started racing across the study. Suddenly, Ankur could no longer feel his body weight, and felt that he was floating.

"What is happening to me, am I dreaming or is this the reality? Did I even have that phone call with Mal, or was I dreaming about that too? I desperately wish that all of this is a dream, and when I open my eyes, I find my Mal asleep beside me", said Ankur, as he was constantly trying to get a grip over his mind and his situation.

"Let me go backwards, let me think! I can do this!".

As soon as Ankur started pressurizing his mind, the barrier between his conscious and his sub-conscious was beginning to tear. He felt as if every action that he had taken in the last few days began playing in front of him!

Ankur had imagined this moment all his life. The moment when he would have finally unlocked the Mental Castle. In his head, he saw the Mental Castle as an all-white replication of the Rajaji Palace where he had grown up. With the same beaming pillars and astonishing architecture, the brick walls were just painted white, like they had been made of sangmarmar. Spanning across the vast walls of the palace, were the memories of Ankur, catalogued from the past to the present. An Ankur used to run across the palace when he was a kid, he could run across his Mental Castle and find the memory he was seeking for, getting complete and reliable information.

Truth, however, is always stranger than fiction. While Ankur could access every memory from the last few days, nothing was catalogued, nothing was segregated, and everything was chaotic. He saw himself standing in front of the dining table and mixing the medicine in the glass of water. Concurrently, he saw himself shouting on the phone in his study, all while he saw himself breaking down the crib with his own hands when Mallory told him she did not want to have a child. Ankur saw the pressure that he was putting on Mallory on that dining table, completely unempathetic of what she was going through.

While Ankur's research was always adamant of finding ways to reach the Mental Castle, he never really had an exit strategy. Every mistake that he had committed over the last few days, played continuously in front of him, becoming more nuanced and hyperbole after every loop.

"Isn't this how our brains function as well? Visiting a memory again and again often magnifies its impact, whether the memory is good or bad", Ankur wondered to himself. "But then, why is it that the bad memories always stick, and the good ones are so easily forgotten."

"GUILT", said Mallory staring at him from the dining table. Ankur knew his mind was now playing games with him, but also providing answers as a reward.

"We overthink and remember our nightmares, because they bring with them, a sense of guilt", said Mallory in Ankur's head.

"I could have stopped the dacoits from killing my family, and I could have stopped Mallory from leaving. I shouldn't have mixed the medicine without letting Mallory know, she would never forgive me now", Ankur was slowly descending into a guilt spiral in his mind, with the replay of every memory in his head.

Ankur had started his research on eidetic memory because he saw the power of not forgetting as a sword that he had used to bring justice to his family. However, today, with everything transpiring continuously right in front of his eyes, he realized how much he had underestimated the power of forgetting.

"I had always seen our capability to forget as a curse, a trait that would be wiped off with years of slow adaptation and gene mutation. But it was a boon. It was a boon that has helped humanity maintain its sanity over the years. I need to find a

way to get out of this! I need to find reality and hold on to it", said Ankur, as he closed his eyes and sat on the floor of his study.

CHAPTER ELEVEN

WINE

Three empty bottles of 'Jacob's Creek Unvind Riesling' rolled on the floor of the observatory. Mallory and Vayu's night was blurrier than the farthest stars. As Mallory's hand bumped into one of the bottles, the bottle rolled down to the observatory's corner.

"What the hell happened last night?", Mallory wondered with no recollection of her night with Vayu.

As she saw the bottle rolling into the corner, it stopped on an item of clothing, which appeared to be Mallory's jeans. As the horror of what had happened set into her eyes, Mallory slowly started sliding her fingers down her neck, realizing that she was completely naked. She quickly got up and glanced around the observatory. The only thing that accompanied her, were her undressed clothes, empty wine bottles, and a truckload of guilt.

Around fifty meters away, Vayu stood in the kitchen, humming his favorite song as he prepared breakfast for Mallory.

"I have just had the best night of my life", Vayu exclaimed to himself as he tossed the omelet into the air from the frying pan. "She is so great, so beautiful, and loves astronomy to her core. It is so rare to find someone like her, especially in today's time".

"But wait, she is also married. Am I a bad person?", thought Vayu as he poured orange juice in a glass.

"Who cares! Her husband does not value her, nor does he understand her. Only an astronomer can understand her, like me!", Vayu excitedly toasted two pieces of bread.

"I mean, it's possible that the world might end in a few months. In front of that, who cares about a drunken night. But what if she sees this as a mistake?", Vayu wondered to himself as he sauteed some pieces of mushroom.

"What the hell am I doing sautéing mushrooms! I should be there once she wakes up! I need to be there when she wakes up!", said Vayu, as he hurriedly plated the breakfast.

"I need to convey to her that there is no pressure to be taken from what had happened last night. If she wishes to go back, she can just think of this as a drunken mistake, I will never even mention it. But what if she wishes to stay? Imagine a world, where she would want to stay", Vayu kept murmuring to himself, as he raced across from his house to the observatory.

"Do you ever wonder if we are made of the same stars?", asked Mallory, as she looked at Vayu with love.

"What do you mean Mal?"

"If we rewind back to the origin of the universe, to the big bang, the originating event only created the simpler elements of the universe, mostly hydrogen and helium.", said Mallory as she reached to Vayu, and held his hands.

"Imagine, every other element that makes you and me, was created in the hearts of stars and was released into the universe when they burst in a supernova explosion. Do you ever think we are all made from the same stars?", asked Mallory looking deep into Vayu's eyes.

"I don't know Mal. All I know is, that *the thought that we have been here, adjacent to each other, for billions of years, is the most beautiful thought I can ever think off*", said Vayu, as he bumped into the gate of the observatory, and the glass of orange juice fell from his tray on the ground.

"Get out of your head, you idiot!", exclaimed Vayu as he realized he was daydreaming. "Act calm, not desperate!"

As Vayu wide opened the gate, the orange juice droplets searched the entire observatory. As Vayu looked around the observatory, the only things that accompanied him, were empty wine bottles, spilt orange juice, and a heartbreak.

CHAPTER TWELVE

CHISELED

The water in the sink ran continuously as the man shaved his beard. Running the razor across his face magnified his perfect jawline. As he stepped out of the shower, wrapping a towel around his waist, he entered the kitchen and pulled out the blender from the storage unit in front of him. Humming a song in his head, he turned around to pick up some strawberries to make his morning smoothie. As he picked up the box of strawberries, his jaw dropped at the sight of his sofa!

"What the hell are you doing here? How did you even get in?", asked Vega looking at the stranger on the couch.

"I have had a key to your house for the last five years Vega. Can you relax a bit. More importantly, can you throw on some clothes please?", said the stranger on the couch.

"Finding it a little hard to control ourselves, are we Mallory?", asked Vega jokingly.

"Right! I am not Uncle. Just wear some clothes, make me your hangover smoothie, and come on the couch please", ordered Mallory.

"I generally only join a woman on the couch if they ask me nicely; but to be honest, I am digging this bossy vibe", Vega joked as he actioned jumping on the couch.

"Oh please! Tone down on the flirting and start hustling on that smoothie, I have a lot to tell you".

"Please don't tell me another comet is coming towards our backyard".

"I have taken a comet, pointed it towards me, and have burnt myself. Will you help me with a hose now?", said Mallory irritatingly.

"So, you want to talk about something that is not work related. Your hair is all messed up, and you look like you haven't slept all night. Am I not understanding the joke, or is this serious?", asked Vega concerned.

"It's serious", said Mallory in a deep voice.

Vega rushed across the house, dressed quickly, prepared a smoothie, and sat on the couch.

"What happened boss? What did you do?"

"I fucked up Vega. I made a horrible mistake", said Mallory.

As Mallory narrated the events that had transpired over the last few days, the reality of the situation was sinking in with every word that she conveyed.

"So, did you sleep with this Vayu guy?", asked Vega.

"I am not really sure. I was devastated after the call, and I drank too much. I think I might have initiated the kiss!"

"WHAT. Did you say you initiated the kiss?", said Vega judgingly.

"Yes. I am sorry; I did not mean to. I wasn't in the right space."

"It's not me who you should apologize to, Mallory. You have really screwed up here!", said Vega consoling Mallory.

"Don't you think I know that. That is why I ran away from the observatory in the morning", said Mallory ashamed.

"You ran away? So, you are not even sure if something happened? You did not talk about it at all?", asked Vega concerned.

"I could not face any of it. I was completely naked in the morning; something must have happened! I just had to get out of there. I can't go back there, NEVER!", said Mallory looking down.

"Look at me Mallory. Do you think you have feelings for him?"

"I don't know", Mallory nodded. "I feel like a high schooler!".

Vega got up from the couch, and went to the table.

"Figure out what is happening with you, boss. You need to face it. If not with this random Vayu guy, you need to face it to Ankur. Finish your smoothie quick, I am taking you back to your place.", said Vega as he grabbed his car keys.

"I can't Vega, I just can't."

"Ankur called here last night, asking if any of our friends had an observatory. He must be worried sick Mallory. Let's go!", said Vega as he progressed towards the gate.

"Vega, will everything be alright?"

"Don't worry, if it won't, a comet is approaching to obliterate us all anyway", said Vega as he exited the house.

CHAPTER THIRTEEN

WHITE ROOM

The walls of Rajaji Palace had been painted all white, just like they were made of sangmarmar. As Ankur was slowly gaining his consciousness, he was trying to open his eyes. The room, while not belonging in the Rajaji Palace, was as clean and white, as he had imagined his Mental Castle to be.

"Where am I? What is happening?", Ankur conversed with himself in his head.

Sitting beside him, holding his hand, sat Mallory. As she was fidgeting with her charm bracelet, her eyes were closed, and her face was resting downwards.

"Are you praying?", asked Vega as he came and sat beside her. "Who are you boss? I have never seen you do anything that even resembled praying!"

"A man in this room taught me, that sometimes, along with hope, all it takes is a little bit of faith", she said in a deep voice.

"When did I teach you that?", said Vega jokingly.

Mallory slowly punched Vega, as she broke into tears. "I haven't cried this much in all my life!".

"Just take deep breaths. You remember what the doctor said, right? No mental stress for Ankur!", warned Vega.

"I need to tell him the truth. I cannot lie to him", she said.

"You need to tell him the truth so that you can absolve yourself of the guilt that you are feeling right now. What you did last night was very selfish Mallory. Please don't act more selfishly. The girl I have known for years is better than this. Let his mind heal first", said Vega.

"What do I do till then?"

"Take care of him. Love him. Help him heal", said Vega.

As Ankur finally opened his eyes, he saw the clean white room as a hospital, and Mallory sitting beside him.

"Mal, are you here?", said Ankur as Mallory rushed towards him. "What happened?"

"That is what I want to ask you? I step out of the house for two days, and I come back to you collapsed on the floor?", said Mallory as she hugged Ankur.

"Do you guys need the room?", said Vega winking his eyes.

"And what is he doing here", said Ankur frustratingly pointing at Vega.

"What I provide, my friend, is humorous retreat. Moreover, who do you think carried you from your study to the car? Your frail wife?", said Vega laughing.

"Let me show you how frail I am?", said Mallory as she advanced to punch Vega.

"Chill! But seriously, are you okay Ankur? What happened?", asked Vega sincerely.

"Do you remember my Mental Castle research?"

"Yes of course. Wait, did you finally crack it?", said Vega excitedly.

"Yes, and it was nothing like I imagined it to be. I guess humanity is never meant to breach some lines."

"Don't get all negative now. Tell me, how was it different?", said Mallory.

"I feel like my brain is punctured Mal. I feel like I have lost the entropy of time. Events, they start occurring in front of my eyes, in no apparent order. Like a bad memory, resurfacing in front of me with every breath that I am taking", said Ankur as he tried to get up from the bed.

"Give it time Ankur. You have exposed your brain to immense stress in the last few days. Take things a bit slow, don't think too much, things will be fine", said Mallory as she supported Ankur in getting up.

"Why don't you guys go out somewhere? Take some time off? You can go to my villa in Daman?", said Vega.

"That sounds nice. The last thing I need right now anyway is to go back to my study", said Ankur.

"Perfect then. Will bring you the keys of the property. Take care", said Vega as he exited the room.

CHAPTER FOURTEEN

BLISTERING WORLD

The Celektron 8000, while habituated of witnessing the most distant galaxies, was observing a heartbreak for the second time. The first time was when Vayu was at the sweet age of sixteen.

Born in Nashik, Vayu Srivastava was a man of humble beginnings. While his dad was one of the most renowned scientists of his generation, he had bottled immense anger at how the world had treated scientists in his time. Being an astronomer at heart, Mr Shyam Srivastava wanted to explore his generation's biggest questions in astronomy. However, as the world was falling apart piece by piece, and with the heavy burden on the government to support its citizens for their basic needs, the funding and respect for astronomy was on a constant decline. Even after his groundbreaking creation of the fertility pill, any grant that Shyam was offered was only related to biochemistry.

"Dad, something weird happened today. My astronomy class got cancelled. The school said that they are not teaching astronomy anymore", said a sixteen-year-old Vayu.

"I know son. The government today has pulled all its funding for astronomical research. Consequently, they have also instructed all the schools and colleges to stop teaching astronomy", said Shyam.

"But that makes no sense. Why won't they teach us astronomy anymore?", Vayu inquired.

"Because we lost kiddo. After several failures to colonize other planets, humanity has failed to become a space faring civilization. Meanwhile, in the hope that humanity would have another planet for solace; the striking climate change sirens have been completely ignored by the leaders of the world", Shyam said in a devastated tone.

"Is that why you go on and give so many speeches? Do you even know how people criticize you behind your back? You have earned so much money, so much respect; why do you expose yourself to these things", asked an irritated Vayu.

"Have you even read the book I have written son? Humanity has created a chain reaction with its constant cycle of greed. Within this century, the majority of species on this planet, including humans, would become incapable of surviving due to the sheer rise in heat. My child, we have created a blistering world for the generations that will come after us, and nobody is ready to take the onus of the same", said Shyam overpoweringly.

"But you did not create this world Dad. Why are you ready to take the brunt of it? People cannot digest straight facts. The deadly truth bombs that you drop in your interviews and through your books do not help anyone", said Vayu as he stepped closer to his dad. "They just make people scared and coerce them to go into denial. We need to make the world understand what you are saying, but you need to find a better method", said Vayu handing Shyam his book.

"But I want them to get scared. How can you sit around and do nothing when the world is ending? I don't understand this mindset", Shyam said as he placed the book on the table.

"*To drive change, you need to inspire hope, not fear. You need to instil the fact that the actions of individuals can create a change*", said Vayu as he picked up his father's book.

"Humanity is sailing on a sinking ship, and nobody knows how to fill the large holes that we have created on its deck. These holes are getting bigger every day, with greed and gluttony of people, whose endless consumption can never fill the void that they have created for themselves", Vayu read from the back of the book.

"Who would want to read this Dad? You are not inspiring any change; you are just venting out your anger. The world needs you to be at your best right now, please!", said Vayu trying to convince his father.

"I can't do this anymore son. The future of a society can be predicted by the way in which it treats its academics", said Shyam, as he picked up a bottle of gin in his hand.

For the first time in his life that day, Vayu had felt a heartbreak.

"The approaching comet is analogous to the blistering world. While it may be more imminent, it poses the same threats as climate change did in Dad's time. The way people are acting, especially their denial, the resemblance is uncanny. I need to do something. The people have a right to know!", Vayu murmured while sitting alone in his observatory.

"The future of a society can be predicted by the way in which it treats its academics", the voice of his father was echoing in Vayu's head.

"What should be the approach so that people can digest such threatening information? I need to find a way, otherwise, it's total chaos", Vayu remembered what Vega had said.

Vayu ran from the observatory back to his room. He pulled out his father's old typewriter, blew off the dust from its keyboard, and inserted a fresh piece of paper.

"DATAR VITAE", Vayu wrote on the paper.

CHAPTER FIFTEEN

THE RETREAT

The Hyundai i20 zoomed via NH 48, carrying two lost scientists in its midst. One astronomer, who had lost her place of work; and another researcher, whose research premise had itself betrayed him. For the first time in their lives, Mallory and Ankur did not have a job, or any work to look forward to. As they drove through the highway to reach Vega's villa, they were amazed by the long wait it had taken for them to take this vacation.

"Are you fine now? Does your head still hurt?", asked Mallory while driving the car.

"Not much. I think these margaritas are going to help", said Ankur, sipping from his glass.

"Are you sure mixing alcohol with medicines is advisable?", said a concerned Mallory.

"Alcohol is the medicine my love!", said Ankur as he winked to Mallory and gulped down his drink.

Mallory looked at Ankur lovingly. "Ankur, are we fine?", she asked.

"Yes, we are. But there are some things that I want to talk to you about?"

"I need to tell you something as well! So, after our fight on the phone that day..."

"MAL", Ankur interjected. "Let us slow down, please. There is no hurry. We can talk all we want. Let us just be with each other for now", said Ankur as he held Mallory's hand.

Vega's villa was the perfect retreat for the nerd couple. Away from city lights, it had a huge terrace with small telescopes. Due to the lack of any light pollution, the entire Milky Way was visible from the large comfortable floor beds on the terrace at night. For the day, there was an enormous pool outside, with sun loungers inviting them for an exciting afternoon.

"I could live here, you know. I don't think we should ever consider going back", said Ankur laughingly, as he entered the villa.

"A jobless Ankur is a weird sight to see. I can't believe you are the same guy who used to forget to have lunch every day. How many margheritas have you had?", asked Mallory strictly.

"Seven"

"SEVEN. It is only four in the evening babe", Mallory was shocked.

"I know I have been a bit slow. We had only made seven before leaving the house. Don't worry, I will try my best to cross twenty today. Happy?", said Ankur as he surprisingly threw Mallory into the pool. "You need to keep up darling. You did not drink any margaritas since you were driving. I expect you to match my number in the next hour", said Ankur as he opened their bags and started making new drinks.

By the evening, as several bottles of tequila rolled around the swimming pool, Mallory and Ankur laid beside each other, exhausted by the afternoon they had.

"I had missed this, Ankur. I haven't seen you like this in so long!"

"Me too. I am sorry Mal, for everything that I said on the phone that day. I was devastated, and for some reason, I made you my outlet", confessed Ankur as he hugged Mallory.

"Your words did not hurt much Ankur. What did hurt, was the sincerity in your tone. You really don't believe in the work that I do, do you?", said Mallory as she slightly pushed Ankur away.

"I do. All I wanted was a chance to explain, but my battery died. Once I charged it, you had switched off your phone."

"My phone broke. I did not switch it off. I wanted a chance to explain as well", said Mallory as she looked deep into Ankur's eyes.

"You have nothing to explain my love", said Ankur as he leaned in and started kissing Mallory.

"I do Ankur, you don't understand!"

"I don't want to understand. I don't care. When was the last time we were this drunk Mal, that we could not control our actions!", said Ankur as he leaned in and started kissing Mallory more passionately.

The empty rolling bottles of tequila transformed into wine bottles. The image of them rolling in the observatory stuck into Mallory's head, as she pushed Ankur away and ran inside the house.

CHAPTER SIXTEEN

DATAR VITAE

Vayu stared at the piece of paper for hours. DATAR VITAE, these are the only words he could summon using his hands.

"Master Vayu, do you need me to get you anything?", asked a voice in a concerned tone. "MASTER VAYU!"

It took Vayu a while to register the source and the nature of the voice.

"Nothing, Ashok!"

"Are you fine sir? You look extremely tense!", said Ashok.

"Yes, I am fine. Please don't worry. Just trying to write something"

"Is someone following the footsteps of his father?"

"NO!", said Vayu angrily. "You know the conflict I and Dad had about his book."

"I understand that you did not believe in his method. But whether you accept it or not sir, you have inherited the disgust your father had with the treatment towards the scientists", said Ashok.

"I know. But you can't just go out and say that a bomb is going to explode. Delivery of information makes a huge impact on the way it is perceived", said Vayu.

"I agree with that. I had even asked Shyamji not to make things so direct. But it was his choice."

"Now I remember. Did you not help dad with publishing?", asked Vayu.

"I did. Proofreading and publishing"

"So, you proofread the entire thing? Why is a learned man like you a house help, Ashok?", asked Vayu.

"Shyamji paid better than a lot of job opportunities that were available in my time sir. Also, I really admired his work. His fertility pill is the entire reason I have a daughter today!"

"Dad's work did leave an impact on people's lives. I don't know what I am doing with mine?"

"Don't worry sir! Your biggest breakthrough is just around the corner. I can feel it."

"I can't. You can go ahead and sleep Ashok", said Vayu as he started staring back at the piece of paper.

"When people start believing that we live in a post-apocalyptic world, there is only so much comfort that scientific principles can provide them. They need to believe in a higher power. They need to believe, in a new higher power", Vayu's eyes shined as his brain processed the idea that was navigating in his head. In an instant, he rolled down the paper and started typing.

"I am DATAR VITAE, the provider of life. For centuries, humanity has believed in archaic structures, and it has gotten them nowhere. Your gods can no longer save you. The world that your god used to wander, even they cannot recognize it now. The death and destruction that humanity has caused to the delicate fabric of this world, your creator could not have even imagined it. The only one who can save humanity is the voice from the sky. It is the voice of a power that has seen it all, sitting distantly far away; every misstep that mankind has ever taken to destroy this planet, every greedy act that mankind committed thinking itself to be the master of its world. While I believed that it was not my place to interfere; today, I must. I speak through the writer of this book. He who writes, speaks for me. Answer him, obey him, and I shall replenish you of all your sins. I shall give your woman the power to conceive again. I shall give your planet, a new breath of fresh air. What I demand in return, is a simple promise. A promise, that you will take better care of the world that you inhabit. But to get another chance, your nascent species will have to go through a test!"

The words for the book were flowing through Vayu's head, like the comet in the sky. He wrote constantly for entire two days, without any rest! All that accompanied him, were small patches of food and water that Ashok used to bring up periodically. At the end of the second day, Vayu was now becoming cognizant:

"What had happened to me? How did I write this entire thing?", Vayu wondered to himself.

"It was divine intervention, sir! Nobody can write with the focus and method in which you have written for the last two days. There is only one explanation; the divine intervention!", said Ashok, sitting in the corner of the room.

"What are you doing here Ashok? Also, there is no such thing as divine intervention. This was just a small stint at hypergraphia. That is all!", said Vayu, as he got up from his seat.

"But sir, did you finish your entire book?", asked Ashok.

"I think so. But there is a high chance it might be garbage. Things written in hypergraphia often lack the meticulousness of a great body of literature. Anyway, I can't sit anymore, my back hurts like hell. I will pick this up whenever I wake up. Good night, Ashok!", said Vayu as he laid down on the bed and went to sleep instantly.

The table lamp lit the white pages of the book, that were stacked beside the typewriter on Vayu's desk. Ashok got up from the corner of the room and slowly progressed towards the desk. As Ashok started reading, the pages slowly changed their colour from white to golden.

"Divine intervention", Ashok said to himself, as he collected the manuscript and left the room

CHAPTER SEVENTEEN

THE TRUTH

Vega's villa had now become habituated of the mild awkwardness that the new resident permanent roommates had brought with them. At one end, was Ankur, tirelessly decorating the terrace of the villa for their special date night!

"Flowers, scented candles, stars, wine; I think I have everything that I need for a perfect date night", Ankur murmured to himself as he carefully placed the flowers and the candles in an ordeal fashion on the terrace. "I don't understand what is happening, it's been more than a week since we have been on this vacation! We have had fights before, but there is something extremely wrong this time. I need to fix this!".

On the other end, was Mallory, stuck in the master bedroom's washroom, giving herself a lousy pep talk.

"You can do this Mallory Shah. You can do this. It has been more than a week; you need to tell Ankur the truth. He is in such a good mood nowadays; we are on vacation; you will not get a chance like this again. Today, you throw on a beautiful dress, you walk upstairs, and you just spit out the truth!", Mallory murmured to herself, with only the villa there to judge her.

As Ankur was adjusting every minute detail of the terrace, he saw Mallory entering in a beautiful black slit dress.

"Today is the day buddy! Today you are getting lucky!", Ankur excitedly poured two glasses of wine and advanced towards Mallory.

"Is that wine?", Mallory asked.

"Indeed, it is. It's Jacob's Creek Unvind Riesling, I saved the best for the last", said Ankur excitedly as he handed Mallory the glass of wine.

"NO; we don't drink wine anymore", Mallory said feverishly. "Do we have anything else left, could you get something else please?".

"Sure Mal", said Ankur diligently, as he ran downstairs to get something else.

"Things cannot go on like this Mallory. You need to tell him. You need to tell him tonight!", she said to herself.

"Hey Mal, did you hear about this guy who is all over the internet!", said Ankur as he entered the terrace with a bottle of gin.

"Who? I don't have my phone remember?"

"There is a guy, he is everywhere. He has published a book. He says that a new almighty god is speaking to us through him! People are also believing him."

"What rubbish. This is my problem with religious people, they have become so weak that they will literally believe in anything."

"It's not weakness Mal. This is how every religion ever has begun. Didn't Allah speak through Prophet Muhammad? Wasn't Jesus the child of God? Didn't Valmiki narrate the story of Lord Ram? The guy might have some plausibility; let us at least keep an open mind!", said Ankur as he sat close to Mallory. "Want to give it a read?"

"I don't open my mind to any of this crap. The simple explanation is that he must be in a deep flow state and was accessing parts of his memory that he wasn't consciously aware of. With your research background, at least you should condemn these things Ankur", said Mallory, chucking Ankur's phone away.

"All that I have learnt from my research Mal, is that the human mind is more complicated than what we can imagine. My research has given me the appetite to give every theory out there a chance!", said Ankur as he held Mallory's hand.

"Ankur, I need to tell you something! Can we please concentrate on us for a second?", said Mallory as she grabbed Ankur's hand more tightly. "That night", she continued, "that night when we..."

Mallory suddenly stopped speaking. A thick rush of fluid filled her mouth, which she immediately spilt out on Ankur's pants. Mallory retched as she had never retched before in her life.

"Shit!", Ankur got up instantly. "Are you okay Mal?"

"Yes", she said gasping for air. "I don't know what happened."

"Don't worry, you have had a lot to drink. It can happen to anybody", Ankur quickly rushed and grabbed Mallory a towel. He then carried her to the washroom downstairs, and sat outside the door, "I am right outside Mal, let me know if you need anything".

"I am so sorry Ankur, I am so sorry", Mallory started crying inconsolably.

"It's just vomit Mal. There is nothing to be sorry about. What is going on with you?"

"Not just the vomit Ankur. I have been a really bad wife. I am a very filthy woman", said Mallory retching in the washroom.

"You are not filthy my love. I haven't been a great husband either. You remember the day you left; I had mixed the fertility pill in the water that you keep in your bedside table", said Ankur sitting outside the door.

An eerie silence filled the room.

"Please forgive me, Mal. I had thought that I would convince you to drink it, but you had already slept. I had just kept it there with the intention that I would convince you to have it in the morning", Ankur continued explaining himself, but the eerie silence from the other end continued.

"Come on Mal, say something. PLEASE!", Ankur shouted as he tried to open the washroom door, which was suddenly bolted from inside.

Mallory stood in front of the sink, feeling that the entire Earth had slid past beneath her legs. As she was slowly digesting the words Ankur had said, along with the pool of vomit that lay in front of her, the horror of reality was slowly setting in. With nothing else that she could do at that moment, Mallory continued retching, as a concerned Ankur kept knocking on her door.

CHAPTER EIGHTEEN

DIVINE INTERVENTION

As Vayu's eyes opened, he could see the fan above him swinging at full speed. Trying to recollect where he is, he quickly tossed around the bed to get a hold of his phone.

"Twenty-three missed calls? All unknown numbers? What is happening? How long was I passed out for?", Vayu kept wondering to himself as he checked the time. He realized that he had had a good seventeen hours of rem sleep.

"That is a long sleep, even by my standards. ASHOK, please get me a cup of coffee", Vayu called out with all the energy that he could gather.

"I have it ready for you sir!", Ashok rushed inside Vayu's room with a cup of coffee in hand.

"What happened to you, Ashok? You look like hell. Did you not sleep last night?", Vayu inquired.

"No, my master. I saw that you had fulfilled your destiny. I just wanted to fulfil mine!", Ashok said as he grabbed Vayu's legs.

"What is going on? I am not your master, and please let go of my legs", said Vayu instantly getting up from the bed.

"You are no longer the man you were sir. You have now become the trinket through which a god speaks to us, lowly creatures."

"Have you smoked something, you idiot? What is going on, tell me clearly."

Ashok rushed outside the room and came back with a book in his hand. DATAR VITAE read the title of the book.

"Did you publish my book without asking me? HOW DARE YOU", Vayu said furiously.

"It was not your permission to give my master like the words were not yours. You are only the funnel through which DATAR VITAE has communicated his wisdom to us mortals. You are the saviour sir. This was your life's purpose", said Ashok as he again fell on Vayu's legs.

"YOU IMBECILE. Have you lost your mind? They were my words. I had written them myself", Vayu's fury with Ashok was rising.

"Do you remember everything that you have written sir? I read your entire book in one go, not a single grammatical error. Not even a single punctuation was placed incorrectly. No man is so precise and so fast at the same time my master, believe me, this is divine intervention."

"How did you even get a publisher to publish something so quickly?"

"Who would have the audacity to deny publishing the next Bible, Geeta, or Quran my master. Every bookstore in the country today will have your book. The entire world would be waiting to hear from you."

"I don't have anything to say to the world, Ashok. Why don't you understand this?"

"Not you sir! You are just the funnel. The entire world awaits to hear from the DATAR VITAE!"

"There is no DATAR VITAE. Shut up! Call your publisher and stop the publishing immediately. This is my copyright!", Vayu was getting angrier at Ashok.

"Then what about the test sir? Sooner or later, the entire world would be ready to perform the test, and you would have to lead it!", said Ashok.

"WHAT TEST?!", Vayu's anger was now accompanied by a truckload of confusion.

"Sir! Looking at you, having no recollection of the book you have written with your own hands, has made my resolve in DATAR VITAE much stronger", said Ashok as he started flipping the pages of the book and handed it to Vayu.

"I sit amongst the stars, watching humanity devour its planet. I see wisdom in the eyes of some great thinkers, but your societal and economic construct does not allow those great ideas to survive. A Beaming Comet is being sent your way, exactly seventy days from the date of publication of this book. If humanity foregoes all its differences and comes together with a promise to take better care of what it takes for granted today, the comet shall keep everyone safe whose heart is pure. If humanity fails, and the beaming comet notices even a slight hint of greed, it shall obliterate everybody in its wake, absolving humanity from the pain of a slow extinction", read the words in the book.

Vayu stared at the book for several minutes and then collapsed back on his bed.

"Sleep tight my master, the great voice of DATAR VITAE", said Ashok as he took the book and left the room.

CHAPTER NINETEEN

CONFIDENTIALITY

The Hyundai i20 zoomed back from Daman towards Mumbai. The disgruntled couple sat in the car, completely still and silent. As Ankur drove the car, Mallory kept researching on Ankur's phone. 'Datar Vitae', she typed on Google search.

"We need to complete our conversation, Mal. Will you please talk to me?", requested Ankur.

"There is nothing to talk about Ankur. Please just keep driving. We need to reach Mumbai as soon as we can", said Mallory, engrossed on the phone.

"Would you look at me while we are talking, please? I am sorry. It was a rash decision that I took in a weak moment. But there is nothing that has gone wrong. We will try and conceive only after the comet passes!"

"Is that why you had decorated the terrace with flowers? Is that why there were scented candles, and wine the other night? What is it with you men and wine!", Mallory exclaimed.

"What do you mean?", Ankur enquired.

"Nothing. I don't have the mental capacity to deal with this now, we need to get to my office immediately. Bigger things are at stake"

"Bigger than us?", Ankur asked slowly.

"There is no place for a love story on a planet that gets blown up Ankur. Just please drive", said Mallory sarcastically.

Ankur, with devastated eyes, stared at the road as he kept driving.

The entire layout of IAA's office had changed after being transferred for medical research. What remained constant, was an array of tensed employees, racing past the bullpen.

"Vega, did we get in touch with Vayu?", asked Chandrakant.

"No boss. No reply from him. His house is also a media circus at this point. No way of contacting him without the state's support", Vega answered.

"Using state's intervention means accepting that we had an idea about the comet. You know we cannot do that. People will crucify us. What about Mallory? What is her ETA?", Chandrakant asked.

"She should be here any minute. Is Uncle planning to take any action against Vayu?", Vega asked.

"Uncle can't. As an intern, he did not sign a confidentiality agreement. Honestly, I don't think even Uncle was expecting us to discover anything that was even worth keeping confidential", Chandrakant answered.

"What is happening Chandrakant?", said Mallory as she entered the room. "What is the plan of action?"

"We need to devise one. People across the globe have started looking for something that resembles what Vayu has described as the beaming comet", said Chandrakant as he took a seat.

"We know what people are going to find. We know they will know the truth", Mallory stepped closer to Chandrakant.

"It is not the truth that scares me, Mallory. It is the chaos that would expedite with every other discovery claiming the knowledge to be true. How do you think people will react once they find out about the comet? ", said Chandrakant.

"It is not just about the comet anymore Chandrakant. Vayu has given this a religious connotation. You know how fanatical people get when a messiah is interconnected to a world-ending event. This is going to be much bigger than we could have ever imagined.", said Mallory.

"A private association in America has identified the claimed comet impact to be true. Vayu's Datar Vitae has just gone global", said Vega from across the room.

"Did they mention the probability of impact?", asked Mallory.

"Eleven per cent, its increasing boss", said Vega.

"Chandrakant, we should get our equipment back, talk to Uncle. We cannot sit like empty ducks", said Mallory.

"We have no option, Mallory. This is how it is now. Vayu has played the last hand, and only he can reverse it. Will you and Vega go and talk to him? See if you can get him to tell everyone the truth?", asked Chandrakant.

A sense of horror set on Mallory's face. The last thing she could afford to do now was to face Vayu.

"I can go talk to him alone, Chandrakant", Vega interjected looking at Mallory's face.

"NO. I think you both should go. Immediately. The news has gone global now, we have very little time", said Chandrakant as he exited the room.

CHAPTER TWENTY

CONFRONTATION

As Mallory and Vega were driving to Vayu's residence, Mallory was facing personal and professional turmoil. Ever since Ankur had mentioned the fertility pill, Mallory had realized that she had some tough confrontations ahead of her.

"Are you okay boss? I understand if you don't want to come. I can do this alone. Let me drop you home", said Vega.

"I need to do this. I may be the only person who can reason with him at this point. This is much bigger than my personal conundrum."

"Did you tell Ankur?"

"I couldn't Vega. There is just so much happening, I just couldn't."

"I can see that. Nausea, vomiting, fatigue. This is not just mental pressure, is it Mallory?"

"Are you out of your mind? This has to be mental pressure; it cannot be anything else."

"I am suggesting that just in case what I am thinking is true, there is a huge confrontation waiting for you at the residence as well", said Vega as he pointed to Vayu's residence.

"Take the route towards the back. I know a way in which we can beat the press", said Mallory pointing.

"Of course you do", winked Vega.

Vayu was racing back and forth, seeing the magnitude of press that stood outside his residence. With no answers to their questions, and nobody to seek advice from, Vayu felt trapped in his own home.

"You son of a bitch!", Mallory entered from behind. "How could you do this? How dare you?"

"Relax Mal, chill. I did not mean for any of this to happen!", Vayu defended himself.'

"Just say her full name my friend, otherwise you might not even survive to see how this pans out", said Vega.

"Explain yourself, you coward jerk", said Mallory.

"Not only did you break the promise of the association, but you have betrayed our trust as well", interjected Vega.

"Look at what is happening out there. You have created a frenzy. Who will take the responsibility?", Mallory interjected.

"Stop tag teaming against me, guys. Let me tell you how all this happened. Please!", Vayu requested.

"You have five minutes", said an angry Mallory.

"And it better be good", said an angry Vega as he threw a chair towards Vayu for him to sit on.

"I knew we could not tell people about the comet. I knew that telling them that there is a possibility that we all might die, would create a purge-like situation, total anarchy", started Vayu.

"Then why did you, you stupid man", interjected Mallory.

"Let me complete. What if we are not obliterated by the comet? What happens in that scenario?", asked Vayu.

"Everybody is safe, and people can go on with living their lives", said Vega.

"Exactly! Tell me honestly Vega, is everybody really safe? Is this comet the only life-threatening event that we are witnessing in front of us? It might be the most imminent, but the way our planet is being defaced; sooner or later, humanity will go extinct if we don't take solid action. The point of the book is to convince people to take this solid action", explained Vayu.

"Did you fall and hurt your head as a child?", said Mallory sarcastically. "What the hell are you even talking about?".

"Wait, Mallory. It does make sense to some extent. If the comet comes and annihilates us, we are helpless anyway. But if it doesn't, why not convince people that it was an act of God? A safety that has been awarded for our promise to keep the planet safe; to make things right. That would convince people to take solid action. It is something that could really save us!", said Vega patting Vayu on the back. "How did you even pull this off Vayu?"

"I had my ways", said Vayu as he winked towards Vega.

"These are people Vega, not his personal puppets on whom he can run these experiments. I cannot believe you are on board with his crazy idea. People's faith is a very delicate instrument to play with, even an atheist like me understands that", said Mallory.

"It is better than not doing anything and watching the world burn Mallory", said Vega as he stepped beside Vayu. Mallory shared a look of disappointment with Vega, turned back in anger, and exited the room.

COLONY

On one side of the house, little droplets of water slowly fell from the tap in the bathroom, overflowing from the already full bucket; on the other side, the pressure cooker was releasing steam in all its glory; on the third, laid a small almirah with twenty-two sections, eleven for clothes, and eleven for medicines, all overflowing; and on the fourth, laid eleven beds side by side, with ten occupants in deep sleep, and one old grandpa shouting with all the energy he could gather:

"WATER! CHILD! WATER!"

"I am coming, learn to wait a bit. It's not like you are going anywhere", came a voice from outside.

Situated at the centre of this chaos, stood Kiara. While just in her early teens, Kiara had more wisdom than all the sleeping oldies in the corner of the house. She quickly turned off the stove and ran from the kitchen with a bottle of water in her hand.

"Here you go!", said Kiara as she extended the bottle to the old man. "Learn to have patience".

"When did I say I needed water? I was trying to say that the water is overflowing in the bathroom", said the old man with a grin on his face.

"Someday, I will ensure that this bed gets empty you old man; and I will distribute all your medicines to the rest of the oldies", said Kiara with a sarcastic tone as she ran towards the tap to close it.

"Even the sweet arthritis ones?", he asked.

"Especially the sweet arthritis ones. I will pop a few myself as a reward for a job well done", said Kiara as she broke into laughter. "I am going out to get some essentials. Will you watch the fort for me?"

"If someone comes and steals something, all I will be able to do anyway is watch. If you want that, sure!", said the old man as he winked at Kiara.

"You can always kill him with your archaic humour!", said Kiara laughingly as she left the house.

Kiara walked on pale congested roads of the infamous Mumbai slum. What was once evidence of the great economic disparity in the country, today stood as a witness of a great age disparity. The average age of the people in this slum in Mumbai, like nearly every other slum in the country, stood at the sweet number of fifty-seven. While it could have easily crossed the sexy number of sixty, a few young residents of the slum like Kiara helped maintain the number in a sweet spot.

"Why are you here again?", said the grumpy store manager as he saw Kiara.

"It is definitely not to see your annoying frog-like face. What is your problem?"

"These old people in your house. They don't have the energy to do anything, they require a thousand medications to even get up from their beds; yet, they inhale food like they are at war. Where does all their energy go?", asked the store manager.

"Not sure about them, but mine goes in tolerating your grouchy tone every morning. See, you have made me hungry. Please fill the bag, would need these items to digest your future complaints", said Kiara as she extended the bag to the manager.

As the shopkeeper began filling up the bag, a flying glass bottle came into the shop slightly touching Kiara's ears. A bewildered and frightened Kiara turned backwards, to see a riot break out in the middle of the narrow street. As the rioters started running towards the store, the manager held Kiara's collar intensely and quickly pulled her inside the shop. As he hurriedly closed off the shutter of the shop, Kiara could see more bottles being pitched towards them. As the shutter closed and the room fell inherently silent, Kiara could hear her own heartbeat.

"Why does this happen every day Santosh? You ration out the essentials adequately for the entire colony. Every house gets its fair share. Then why do people riot to get more? Why do humans want to hoard things that they cannot utilize?", asked Kiara, holding her ears tightly to stop the blood flow.

"What if the store stops getting supplies tomorrow, my dear? What if someone wants to have one extra piece of chapati? You can call it greed, or hoarding, or ambition for a better life; but the need inside us that drives this nomenclature, has been present in humans since the very beginning", said Santosh as he tended to the wound in Kiara's ears.

"Would God not condemn this? How can we pray in the morning and destruct in the evening?", asked Kiara.

"Like everything else in this universe, our relationship with God is also a cause-and-effect relationship. We all have different levels of faith because there are different levels of

expectation that we set for our lords. While a more religious bunch, like us, will suffice with small tinkers of hope, the atheist scientists out there tend to generally require much more proof", he said. "Similarly, the people that you see outside, they pray every morning, with a new hope that someone out there will listen. By evening, when they do not get any answer back from the universe, they destroy".

"What can we do then?", asked Kiara.

"Wait for the morning. Don't worry, all of us pray at some moment in our lives.", said Santosh as he handed Kiara a piece of small binoculars.

"What is this", she asked.

"The next time you look up at the sky to locate God, use these binoculars. You will feel him a little bit closer", said Santosh.

CHAPTER TWENTY-TWO

DEVOTION

A panting Mallory ran across the narrow lanes of Mumbai. After a betraying friend, a deceitful husband, a careless boss, and a devilish one-night stand, she found herself alone on the roads of Mumbai, trying to stop a religious revolution.

"ASHOK, ASHOK", Mallory shouted around the lane, asking every passing person if he had ever come across the name.

"Do any of you know Ashok? It is very important for me to meet him, please!", Mallory requested a passing man.

"Relax my child! I know you are in search of Datar Vitae. But Ashok is not the messenger", said an old man by putting his hand on Mallory's head.

"Who said I am searching for Datar Vitae? There is no such thing as Datar Vitae", shouted Mallory, as she heard the entire road gasp. Suddenly, every person was looking at Mallory. From an irrelevant stranger shouting on the road, she had become a culprit with a target on her back.

"People's faith is a very delicate instrument to play with", she remembered to herself. "I need to find Ashok. I am a friend of Vayu; I have worked with him. Please take me to Ashok. I have more information to give him!", she pleaded to the public.

"What information?", a man with dark eyes came and asked Mallory.

"The date and time of impact. Datar Vitae has communicated the exact date and time of impact", Mallory said nervously.

"But I thought he did not exist for you?", taunted a stranger from an adjacent shop.

"I had to check if everybody here was a real believer. Instructions from Mr Vayu himself", said Mallory shakingly.

"I will take her to the master. He will decide if there is any truth in what she speaks", said Salud, as he grabbed Mallory's hand and instructed her to start walking forward.

As Mallory walked through the narrow lanes of Mumbai, she could not recognize the city in which she had lived her entire life. The slums of Mumbai were known to be jacked up with old men and women, who used to get subsidized food and medicines and would never leave their bedside for anything. Today, it felt as if the entire slum was out on the streets.

"What is everybody doing? Why are they out here in the open?", asked Mallory.

"What do you mean in the open? This is where we live!", said Salud.

"I meant; doesn't the dependent population just stay back at their quarters? The government assigns young volunteers specific quarters to help them, right?", she asked.

"It's not often you get a message from a messiah. Now is no time to rest, now is no time to be dependent. Every person needs to pull their weight. This is the only way for us to pass the test", he said.

"But what weight do we even need to pull? I mean, is this test not simple enough? We just need to stand in one place, and promise that we would take better steps."

"You speak like a woman who has no faith. A person who has no faith has nothing to live by. When God asks you to do something materialistic like pour him gallons of milk, he tests your faith. But, when God asks you to promise and resolve that you will do what is right, he tests your intention. I can tolerate a woman without faith, but I need to ask you ma'am, what are your intentions?", said Salud with his dark eyes staring at Mallory.

"My intention is only to help!", said Mallory nervously. "I just need to speak to Ashok".

"Your intentions do not seem pure. But it is not my place to judge. In a few days, Datar Vitae will judge", said Salud as they reached a giant wooden door.

"You will find the master in there. He does not answer to Ashok, only to master. Be careful madam, the judgement day is upon us, and Datar Vitae will know your intentions", said Salud as he pounded on the door, turned around, and left.

As the gate fell ajar, Mallory slowly pushed the gate. "Ashok, are you there?" she said nervously as she opened the door.

"No, he is not; and he is master, not Ashok", said a girl sitting alone in the room, with tiny binoculars around her neck.

CHAPTER TWENTY-THREE

INFORMATION

After carefully tucking in all the eleven oldies in their beds, Kiara proceeded towards the terrace for her favourite time of the day. When you spend all your life in cluttered rooms and chaotic streets, the vastness of the cosmos gives you unimaginable comfort. As she slowly picked up her tiny binoculars to see if God seemed to be closer to her in space, she heard a big scream downstairs.

"KIARA! KIARA!", shouted a man as he entered the house.

Kiara jumped from the terrace, frightened to her core. Standing before her, was her father in flesh and blood. But in spirit, Ashok was a completely different man. Known across the colony for his patience and calm demeanour, Ashok today had no reason to be patient and calm.

"Look at this. My master! My master Vayu! God is speaking through him! God talked to him! He can talk to God", Ashok kept stammering and murmuring to himself, as he collapsed on the floor.

The grumpy grandpa with arthritis slept with a grouch on his face, as he had to share a bed with Ashok that night. But while Grandpa was finding a perfect position for a good night's sleep, Kiara was finding her purpose. After carefully tucking Ashok in the bed, Kiara went back to the terrace and started reading the book Ashok had brought with him.

"Datar Vitae speaks through master Vayu. But Datar Vitae speaks to ME", Kiara said to herself after dissolving herself in Vayu's book.

"Datar Vitae also speaks to ME", said a stranger standing in front of the house.

"How can you hear me?", Kiara looked down from the terrace of her small house.

"Because Datar Vitae speaks to both of us", the stranger said.

"I don't have time for this nonsense. Please keep walking. When I am so disinterested in speaking with you, why would Datar Vitae be interested?", said Kiara sarcastically as she got back to the book.

"In the book, are you stuck on the test too?", the stranger asked Kiara.

"What is there to be stuck on? It's fairly a simple test", she said.

"Is it?", he asked again.

"If humanity foregoes all its differences and comes together with a promise to take better care of what all they take for granted today, the comet shall keep everyone safe whose heart is pure", Kiara read aloud an excerpt from the book.

"Humanity needs to come together and forego its differences. I must bring everyone together and unite at one place!", Kiara jumped from the terrace excitedly in front of the stranger.

"Well, congratulations! You have successfully untangled a mental knot", he said.

"Mental knot?", Kiara asked confused.

"I am a scientist. I have spent a better part of the last decade researching eidetic memory. In my research, I describe this sudden urge of purpose as untangling a mental knot. We can often feel our purpose in our bones but are unable to find an outlet for it. When we do, we untangle a mental knot!", he said.

"A scientist, and you believe in Datar Vitae?", she asked.

"Einstein was a religious man, why can't I be?"

"I think it is harder to convince scientists of anything. They seem to constantly question everything obvious."

"On the contrary, you should focus on the obvious. If Datar Vitae has sent a comet as a test, find someone who can validate it. If you can validate the existence of the comet, you can validate the existence of Datar Vitae", said the stranger as he turned around and began to leave.

"Why are you leaving? Can't you help me with this?", Kiara asked.

"This is all the help that I can provide. I need to find and talk to my wife. But I believe you will figure it out. Try to find a private organization, preferably in other countries. My father used to say, *information is the most valuable thing in this world, more valuable than diamonds*", said the stranger as he exited the street.

CHAPTER TWENTY-FOUR

BELIEF

"Who are you? I need to speak to Ashok", said Mallory as she entered the room.

"Do you think it's so easy to speak to master? What is it that you want?", asked Kiara furiously.

"I am a colleague of Vayu; the person whose book Ashok has been preaching around the town", said Mallory as she came close to Kiara. "How can you people take something that was his and preach it?"

"Datar Vitae speaks through him, but that does not give him the right to conceal any information. Let me guess, you don't believe in Datar Vitae?", asked Kiara as she stepped very close to Mallory.

"There is nothing to believe. I know that he does not exist!", Mallory said as she took a few steps back.

"Do you know the great power of belief? It can create things out of thin air! If you do not believe in a higher power; I don't care. I believe in Datar Vitae, hundreds of people working outside, they believe in Datar Vitae; because we all believe, Datar Vitae exists!", said Kiara as she went back and sat on the sofa in the room.

"But that makes no sense! Your thinking cannot change reality, believe me. Vayu just wrote this book, out of his own wit, and people like you have been overanalyzing it to another level", Mallory pleaded to convince Kiara.

"But that is what I am trying to explain. Religion might be propagated from any faucet of humanity, but belief can only arise from within. These people who are working outside, are creating shelter and food for the thousands of people that are coming here to witness the comet. Two weeks ago, they could not even get out of their own beds. Belief in anything can change the entire being of a human. Try believing in something for once, and believe me it will exist", said Kiara as she ushered Mallory to come and sit beside her.

"Did you say a thousand people are coming!", Mallory was shocked. "But how did you convince thousands of people to come here and watch the beaming comet?", Mallory asked softly as she sat beside Kiara.

"Do you think I am famous? No. A random stranger on the street gave me the idea of confirming whether the comet was real or not. Master Ashok knew a few old astronomers in America as he had been working with the Srivastava family for so long; and guess what, voila! There actually exists a beaming comet!", said Kiara as she stumbled a few pages and showed a file to Mallory.

"Did you really tell people that a comet is coming? A comet that can potentially obliterate all of us, and people are coming here to celebrate?", said Mallory as she sulked into the sofa.

"You need to present the information in a way people can digest it. Otherwise, its total chaos!", said Kiara.

"This is my friend's line, how do you know it?", said Mallory confused as she rose back again on the sofa.

"The stranger on the street, he said to me", Kiara said,

"Who the hell is this stranger on the street?"

"I am", said Ankur standing at the wooden door.

"Hey! What are you doing here", said Kiara as she hopped from the sofa to greet Ankur. "Did you have any luck finding your wife?"

"He did", said Mallory from the back. Kiara took a minute to digest the domestic tension in the room and awkwardly stepped outside the door.

"Did you give her the idea to talk to a scientist in America? To validate Datar Vitae's test?", asked Mallory disappointingly.

"Mal, what if it's true? What if there is someone out there who is coming to save us? Will you stop fighting this for just one second", pleaded Ankur.

"I will stop fighting this Ankur, because I need so much more energy to fight with you. I can't convey how much you have hurt me in the last few days", said Mallory as she sulked back onto the sofa.

"You have all our lives to tell that to me my love", said Ankur as he came and sat beside Mallory.

"What if the comet comes and hits us?", said Mallory as she held Ankur's hand.

"Vega just called. He has been trying to reach you for hours. They have been tracking the comet from Vayu's observatory for the last few days. It's not going to hit us. It's going to pass", said Ankur as he looked at Mallory, with tears in his eyes.

Mallory leapt and tightly hugged Ankur. "We are going to be safe!"

"Yes Mal, so will our future child. We can finally have the family we had always dreamt of!", said Ankur as he tightly hugged Mallory.

As the horror of a falling comet was slowly fading away in Mallory's head, the horror of her actions was finally settling in.

CHAPTER TWENTY-FIVE

DOOMSDAY

The Hyundai i20 continuously honked the busy streets of Mumbai that saw the inflow of thousands of people from across the country, that had come to witness the beaming comet of Datar Vitae. Inside, sat two scientists. One, a researcher, elated beyond his core, for all his dreams seemed finally aligned with reality after a rough couple of months; another, a dejected astronomer, repenting her past actions and summoning the ability to tell Ankur the truth.

"DATAR VITAE! DATAR VITAE!", chanted the crowd outside.

"I don't think we will be able to move further, Mal. We will have to walk", said Ankur.

"Huh!", a confused Mallory looked at Ankur.

"Are you fine my love? What happened?", asked a concerned Ankur.

"Nothing, I am fine. There is a lot that we need to talk about Ankur", she said.

"Don't worry. After today, we will have our entire lives to talk about whatever you want", said Ankur as he calmly comforted Mallory.

"Need a ride?", a shining black Mercedes pulled beside Ankur and Mallory.

"How the hell does this guy drive a Merc, and his boss drives a Hyundai!", said Ankur jokingly.

"He does not have two mouths to feed, does he?", said a sarcastic Mallory as she got out of the car.

"All my money is from the astronaut days Ankur. If I had to survive on the basis of the salary you get as an astronomer, I would have shot myself twice!", said Vega as he gestured for Ankur to hop in.

"Let me make it easier for you. After today, I will fire the first shot!", said Mallory as she hugged Vega.

"How does it matter if it is a Mercedes or a Hyundai? The crowd is not going to let us drive any further. You realize that right?", said Ankur as he saw a fleet of people standing in front of them on the roads.

"I carry the most effective siren here with me", said Vega as he pointed towards the passenger seat.

"Vayu! I have been intending to meet you for so long!", said Ankur excitedly as he jumped out of the car and ran to greet Vayu. Mallory's face turned pale in an instant.

"Don't worry Mallory. You have all the time in the world now. You can take your time and talk to him. You can sort it out!", said Vega as he held Mallory's hand and guided her to the back of the car.

Vega suddenly pulled out a loudspeaker from beneath his legs, and started announcing.

"VAYU SRIVASTAVA. THE MAN WHO SPEAKS TO DATAR VITAE IS TRAVELLING IN THIS CAR. REQUESTING EVERYONE TO PLEASE LET HIM PASS THROUGH!".

Suddenly, the entire crowd cleared the way for Vega's car to proceed.

Mallory, Vega, Vayu, and Ankur, stood at an elevated stage that was created by the old people in Kiara's slum.

Thousands of people stood beneath, covering the entire marine drive, constantly chanting 'DATAR VITAE'. On high rise hotels that surrounded the lavish Nariman Point, stayed wealthy businessmen, politicians, actors, and other celebrities. The rocks of marine drive were covered with speakers that could shake every drop in the Arabian sea, with a mic attached onto the stage Vayu was standing on. Reporters stood at every nook and cranny that they could find, filming the entire thing. The entire world awaited the beaming comet.

"Do you agree with my methods now?", asked Vayu as he stood beside Mallory on the stage.

"Just because you got away with it, does not mean what you did was right", said Mallory giving a disapproving look.

"One day, a drunk Mallory had asked me what faith felt like! I thought I would give her a view", said Vayu as he gestured towards the chanting crowd.

"You are a sick man! Are you sure the comet is going to pass?", she asked.

"One hundred percent. I calculated the trajectory myself", he said. "Now please excuse me, I need to give a little speech".

"Rub that smirk off your face, otherwise a child seven lanes away will also recognize the fake fraud that you are", said Mallory as she stepped backwards.

"Such inspiring words", said Vayu as he switched on the mic, beginning to make an announcement. The entire crowd in a moment, fell silent.

"One night, I was sitting alone in my study, pondering over my purpose in this world. I saw the destitute beings we had become, and knew that like my father, it must be my path to change the fate of the world. But where my father gained inspiration from the erudite study of science, I was inspired by the powers of a higher being. While my father was tested by small intricacies of a scientific endeavor, I was tested by the power of my faith and belief. But I was not being tested alone. THE DATAR VITAE WOULD COME TODAY AND TEST US ALL!", Vayu shouted as the crowd began screeching at their utmost capacity.

"The beaming comet would come, inspect our true intentions, and absolve us of our past sins. It will pave the way for a bright future for humanity. All we need to do, is cleanse our hearts, and stand strong with our promise", Vayu continued.

"DO WE PROMISE TO MAKE THIS WORLD A BETTER PLACE??!!"

"YES!", the crowd chanted.

"WILL WE RESPECT THE GIFT OF MOTHER EARTH??!!"

"YES!", the crowd screamed higher.

"My friend Vega will count down the beaming comet", said Vayu as he stepped back.

"Could you have made it any cheesier?", asked Mallory as Vayu stepped back from the mic, and Vega started counting down the coming of the comet.

As Vega finished his countdown, a bright light filled the sky in front of them and enlightened the entire Arabian Sea till its horizon. By seeing the angle of the light, the four people on the stage quickly realized that the comet was indeed going past them, albeit very closely. As everyone looked at the sky awed at the presence of the space faring object in their night sky, Mallory suddenly felt something wrong in the silhouette that the light was creating. As the comet went further, a form of terror started setting into Mallory's eyes.

"VAYU, LOOK AT THE LIGHT. SOMETHING IS WRONG!", she shouted and ran towards Vayu.

"Is the comet, is the comet splitting in two parts?", said Vayu as he looked back at Mallory in dread.

What Mallory's experience had allowed her to realize a few moments earlier, was now being witnessed by everyone looking at the comet for blessing. People's intentions weren't so pure after all. As the entire crowd started running in chaos, stampeding the mob that had come to support each other, a tiny piece of the comet broke off and was heading directly for Nariman Point. Up on the stage, Vega and Vayu stood at the front end of the stage, ready to witness the impact they had brought upon themselves. Towards the back, Ankur was shivering constantly, as if the life changing event had unlocked his Mental Castle. In the middle, stood Mallory, realizing that she would not have all the time in the world to fix her mistake.

"Ankur, I need to tell you something", said Mallory as she went towards the back and hugged Ankur tightly.

"I love you too Mal, and I am sorry too", said Ankur as he hugged Mallory back.

"I am pregnant Ankur".

"How is tha...", Ankur stammered.

"I cheated on you. I slept with Vayu after we had our big fight. I did not know you had given me the fertility pill. I am so sorry!", Mallory pleaded to Ankur as she broke down.

Ankur looked above at the approaching comet. Mallory's words had transformed his feeling of desolation into relief.

As the small piece of comet descended towards the crowd, everyone present at the venue accepted their fate. The religious people had accepted that their intentions were not pure enough, and the atheists had accepted the religious joke that was played on them. But, as the comet sped towards the ground for impact, it suddenly slowed, as if deaccelerating on its own. The comet slowed, maneuvered, and placed itself carefully between two rocks at Nariman Point. The small piece of comet, which was now simply a small rock, opened its top hatch and extended a musical instrument, something that strongly resembled a telegraph key with speakers attached to it.

The telegraph key emitted a strong colorful light, completely covering the sky in a beautiful symphony of colors. From left to right, a distinct color filled the sky, a combination of shades which humans had never seen before in their lives. After a mere two seconds of the colorful display, the sky turned back to normal, and a screeching high-pitched noise followed, speaking in dots and dashes.

"IS IT MORSE?", Vayu shouted with the mic still turned on in his hand.

Vayu quickly got up and started decoding the same in his head. The message said:

```
_ _ · _ _ _ _ _ ·
```
G O D
```
· · · · _ _ · · _ _ · _ · · _ · _ _ ·
```
S P E A K I N G

"God Speaking", Vayu said softly on the mic.

CHAPTER TWENTY-SIX

AFTERMATH

As the comet was descending, panic was the common response amongst the masses present at Marine Drive. As the comet had deaccelerated and landed between the rocks, the entire mob stood there, quietly in awe, and saw the small piece of rock manoeuvre. When it hit the ground and extended a telegraph key, the entire crowd was, to say the least, confused; looking up to Vayu for an answer. Slowly, when Vayu translated the Morse code to be 'God Speaking', the entire mob, euphoric on hearing those two words, screamed in unison as they progressed and started running towards the stage.

"What in the name of god is happening?", Vega shouted standing on the stage.

"Don't you dare take god's name right now! Vayu, what the hell did you do", said Mallory demanding Vayu for an answer.

"Was it actually a divine intervention? Can I really speak to God? Why did God choose me?", Vayu kept whispering to himself.

"Get out of your head you idiot. We need to leave right now!", said Mallory pointing towards the mob that was approaching the stage to greet Vayu.

"Why run? They love me, right?", asked Vayu innocently.

"No darling, they worship you! Think about it, which godman has ever survived blind worshipping?", said Mallory as she held Vayu's hand and started running.

As they turned back, they saw Ankur, still shivering and shaking to his core.

"Babe, what is happening to you?", Mallory quickly ran to check up on Ankur.

Ankur stared at Mallory for a moment and then fainted on the stage. With the crowd constantly running towards them, Mallory was looking at a more realistic cause of death for her little group.

"We need to do something!", screamed Mallory.

"Look, are they here to save us?", Vayu pointed towards the sky, which was rapidly filled with state rescue choppers.

The chopper stood at the front of the stage, witnessing two individuals waving their arms towards them. Ignoring them, it dropped two individuals who picked up the small piece of rock, turned around, and left with the remaining choppers.

"WHY DID THEY NOT PICK US UP?", shouted Vayu as he saw all the state rescue choppers leave.

"Because you my friend, contrary to what you have started to believe, are no interpreter of a Datar Vitae. You should pull your socks up, understand that you also have no clue what is happening, and get real about your options", said Vega as he shrugged Vayu and picked a fainted Ankur from the ground.

"No point picking him up Vega, nobody is coming to save us!", a devastated Mallory sat on the ground.

"Quit whining and look up at the sky. An actual saviour is coming this time!", said Vega as he walked towards the edge of the stage.

Two pieces of rope fell from the sky. Vega walked towards one which attached itself to him and pulled him up. Floating above the little group, was a matte black Octacopter.

"Hurry up!!!", shouted the man standing at the gate of the octacopter.

Vayu quickly rushed towards the rope, which refused to attach itself to him.

"It's biologically activated Vayu, it won't attach to you", said Mallory as she walked towards the rope.

"What about me then?", said a frightened Vayu.

"The little guy wants to come as well, should we let him?", asked the man standing at the gate from inside.

"We can leave him here. He wanted to show me what real faith looks like, I would really like to see", said Mallory pointing towards the running crowd.

"You will anyway have to pick him up if you want to bring him along", said the man standing at the gate.

Mallory walked towards the rope which attached itself to her. She stared at Vayu with cold eyes. In return, Vayu looked at her with desperation. Looking at him, she gestured for Vayu to hop on. As he leeched onto Mallory, Mallory slowly pulled down the rope, which launched them abruptly towards the octacopter.

CHAPTER TWENTY-SEVEN

BOSS

The octacopter was an engineering marvel of the twenty-second century. Developed solely for one man by the best engineering company on the planet, it was a flying townhouse in the sky; with a fully equipped clinic, one giant master bedroom, and a boardroom that could host a party of twelve. Most importantly, it was the haven of one of the most influential people on the planet. At the gate, stood a six feet tall mountain of a man, Rashid.

As Vega slid up with the rope, Rashid came and hugged Vega tightly, gesturing towards the clinic where he could lay down Ankur. He then proceeded towards Mallory and hugged her.

"I have had the doctors alerted in the clinic. They will tend to Ankur right away, you please don't worry", said Rashid.

"Do you have a neurosurgeon on board, he might require immediate attention!", said a concerned Mallory.

Rashid gave a solacing look to Mallory. "Just relax and please go inside. You know we have better facilities here than what you can get on the ground!", he said as he gestured towards her to proceed inside.

"Where do you think you are going little man?", said Rashid as he spotted Vayu following Mallory inside.

"What do you mean? I am with her, where am I supposed to go?", said Vayu as he stepped closer to Rashid in the hope of standing his ground.

Rashid quickly held Vayu by his hands, pressed him against the wall, and searched him thoroughly.

"You can now go and sit in the guest room that way", said Rashid pointing towards the room on the side of the gate.

"Let the traitor come in. I need to have a word with him", said a deep voice from inside.

As Rashid stepped out of the way, a puzzled Vayu entered the room. Inside the room, sat a bald man in a three-piece suit, with a grid of nine television screens stacked in front of him, creating one single giant wall of screen. On one hand, he held a glass of whiskey, swirling his hands around the glass. On the other, with a red stoned ring on his index finger, he gestured for Vayu to come and sit beside him.

"Are you, are you Uncle?", Vayu stammered.

"Some people know me by that name. But people that generally do, aren't brave enough to cross me like you did Vayu!", Uncle said in a very serious tone.

"But I-I did not", Vayu continued stammering.

Uncle slowly slid towards Vayu, wrapped his hands around Vayu's shoulder, and pointed towards the screen.

"So, Mr. Vayu Srivastava, who is this Datar Vitae and why does it speak through you?", asked a reporter on the giant nine-screen television.

"Datar Vitae is a being so complex, that our mortal brains cannot fathom its shape, form, or existence. While Datar Vitae does not meddle in the conflicts of lowly beings like us, it is doing us a favour by making an exception. Without his intervention, humanity is assured to slowly go extinct."

"Would you call what you have made, a deal with the devil? Either the Datar Vitae absolves us of all our sins, or it destroys everything in its wake!", asked the reporter.

"A deal is where you have something to give in return. Datar Vitae does not require anything from us. There is nothing we can provide him with. Let me assure you, this is not a deal, this is charity", said Vayu as Uncle pressed the remote and paused him on the screen.

"So, Mr. Vayu. You take information that you received using my equipment, tell it to the entire world, and create a cute little scenario where you can walk away as the voice of the God!", Uncle said slowly.

"What you need to understand Uncle…"

"SILENCE! YOU WILL SPEAK WHEN I ALLOW YOU TOO!", screamed Uncle as he started coughing uncontrollably.

"You are a very lucky man that rats aren't feasting on your dead body right now in the slums, little man", said Rashid as he handed Uncle some water and medicine.

"You will now, without breaking the flow, tell me in a clear and concise manner, what is happening, and what is going to happen next!", Uncle said in a deep voice.

"But I can't sir! I have no clue! Yes, I wrote Datar Vitae with the knowledge that the comet was approaching. But that is all! I don't know anything about what just happened right now", Vayu confessed.

"Mallory! Thoughts?"

"I don't know Uncle. We need to get our hands on the piece of rock as soon as we can. The rock has all the answers!", said Mallory.

"What about him? You trust this piece of shit?", Uncle pointed towards Vayu.

"I am one hundred per cent sure that he is not smart enough to pull this off! He is just lucky", said Mallory.

"I would rather say unlucky! Who knew such a loose prophecy would come true!", said Vayu disappointed.

"Young man! For the first time in your life, you have become a little relevant and have a little power in your hands, be happy. How do you think any prophecy ever comes true? You just need to design it loose enough!", said Rashid.

"But this one is too improbable Rashid. I think we are on the cusp of something, I can feel it. Mallory, I need you to be at your best, okay?", said Uncle.

"Yes Uncle", Mallory nodded.

"How is he as a scientist?", Uncle looked at Vayu with disgust.

"He is actually pretty good!", said Mallory.

"Are you sure you are not just protecting him because he is the father of your child!"

Mallory's face turned pale. Vayu, shocked to his core, instantly jumped from the sofa.

"Relax! What an immature child!", said Uncle as his disgusted expression continued.

"He is actually good! I have seen him!", said Vega from behind.

"Is Ankur okay?".

"Yes Mallory, he will wake up in a few hours"

"GUYS! A piece of rock just came in falling from the sky, literally. A rock that you had been tracing for months. The rock opened, talked in morse, and took god's name. Can we please pause the family drama for a few seconds!", said Uncle as he irritatingly got up from the sofa. "We will reach the location of the rock in an hour, rest however you want! Just be ready to give me answers once we reach there!"

"Did Uncle say we are going towards the rock? The government took it from the site, right?", asked Vayu looking around.

"This guy Mallory. Seriously!", said Rashid with a judgmental look on his face as he exited the room.

CHAPTER TWENTY-EIGHT

INANIMATE

The large barren military land near Dehu Road, Pune, was not accustomed to visitors. With a large perimeter being created across acres of desolate land, a stability test chamber stood in the middle of the perimeter. Up on the octacopter, Mallory sat in the clinic, holding Ankur's hand who had still not gained consciousness. Vayu sat outside the clinic, digesting the information that was just communicated to him. Vega, looking outside the octacopter and detached from all the drama, was looking forward to meeting God!

"I need to fly back to Delhi; the PM is having an emergency conference. By the time I meet him, I am expecting an answer!", said Uncle as was standing at the gate of the octacopter, waiting to drop off the crew on the sensitive military facility.

"Aren't you going with him?", asked Vayu, as he saw Rashid approaching the gate.

"Who is going to keep your betraying ass in check?", asked Rashid as he pushed Vayu from the octacopter.

"Why do you treat him this way? I don't think Uncle was so offended by his book", said Vega to Rashid as he approached the gate.

"The lad is good with people. But at the first opportunity that he got, he transformed himself into a godman. Uncle thinks he is important, but I don't trust his intentions", said Rashid.

"What do you think we will find in the rock?"

"I know you are not a religious man Vega, but the way things have transpired, you cannot deny the possibility."

"No god ever arrives calling himself a god Rashid. I think Vayu might not be the only one whose intentions we cannot trust!", said Vega as he jumped off from the octacopter as well.

"What is the update boss?", asked Mallory as she went and hugged Chandrakant in the stability test chamber.

"This thing is very strange Mallory. It is just easier to show you!", said Chandrakant as he moved towards the centre of the chamber.

An oval-shaped, lustrous box stood in the middle of the chamber, carefully placed inside a glass box.

"This is not the rock that we had seen!", said Vayu.

"The outer layer, resembling a rock, was just for transportation. It came off very easily", said Chandrakant.

"Any signs of abnormal radiation?", asked Vega.

"No. No abnormal radiation and no signs of explosives"

"What is it then? It must be hollow right?", asked Mallory.

"The initial impressions show that it is protecting something inside, but we cannot be sure".

"Let us just break it open then; what is the delay?", said Vayu as he stepped towards the glass box.

"Be my guest. How do you want to break it open?"

"Simple, figure out what is it made of. Looks like an extremely lustrous steel. Did you try melting it?", said Vayu.

"What a novel idea. Of course, we did. We can't seem to break it open. The outer layer is very shiny, but immensely strong at the same time", said Chandrakant.

"I need to inspect by hand", said Vayu as he moved forward, cutting the crowd.

"Where do you think you are going?", said Rashid, as he stopped Vayu from cutting him.

"You won't find answers standing here Rashid. We need to act, and we need to act fast. Let me do this!", said Vayu as he looked back at Mallory. Mallory nodded, and Vayu was sent to suit up for a one-on-one with the lustrous box.

An entire crowd of scientists stood in the barren military land, looking at the box in awe. No human had ever seen something like this in their lives, and everybody in that room knew that no human could ever create it. The religious fraternity was ready to meet their god, and the atheists were ready to get answers to the Fermi Paradox.

CHAPTER TWENTY-NINE

AWAKE

The white walls of Rajaji Palace had returned, and Ankur had grown tired of waking up in an infirmary. To his dismay, this time, even Mallory was not present there to hold his hands. As he saw strange doctors looking at him like he was an alien, he tried to scooch from the hospital bed, attempting to get up.

"Do you remember the last twenty-four hours, sir?", a concerned doctor approached Ankur.

"A bit of it. Why?"

"We have never seen such magnitude of brain activity in an unconscious person", said the doctor. "We would love to run more tests on you if you would allow"

"As much as I am grateful that you deem me worthy of treating as your lab rat, I would like to go back to my wife", said Ankur sarcastically as he made another attempt to get up from his bed.

"Out of everyone, why did you choose that imbecile to go inside Rashid?", Ankur overheard a man outside shouting on his phone.

"UNCLE!", shouted Ankur.

"Tell Mallory her husband is awake. Sending him to the military base back in the octacopter", informed Uncle on the phone.

"How are you feeling young lad?"

"Young, that is not a term that applies anymore to me Uncle. I went unconscious so many times in the last few days, I don't think I can trust my brain anymore", said Ankur.

"Activities of the mind, Ankur, are the hardest to figure out. But you have truly taken on a marvellous endeavour. I don't know how successful you will be with this, but I believe that it is people like you who will change the fate of this world", said Uncle as he got up from the seat near the hospital bed. "You know I am the last to entertain any family drama, but give your wife a chance. The world needs both of you to be at your best", said Uncle as he left the room.

"To be at our best, we need representation from both sides", Ankur wondered to himself as he sat alone in the clinic bed. After some thought, he pulled out his phone and started sending a text to a friend from the other side. 'Military Base, Pune!', the text read.

As Ankur was flying back from Delhi to Pune on the octacopter, the world below him was transforming continuously. Small pockets of radical believers were forming across India and moving towards Pune. With Ashok and Kiara at the forefront for the group from Mumbai, the military facility knew that they would have a tough time protecting the little box that they had tucked away in their stability test chamber.

"Master, are you sure about marching towards Pune?", asked Kiara as the group kept walking in unison.

Ashok nodded.

"Master! Master!", Kiara kept repeating.

"WE WILL REST FOR A FEW MOMENTS", announced Ashok as the crowd sat down.

"Is it wise for us to go towards Pune Dad?", asked Kiara.

"Yes, my child! But, if you are asking me this question as my daughter, and not a believer of Datar Vitae, I can sense your faith shaking!", said Ashok.

"It is not about my faith; I just think that the military and the scientists are looking at the blessing by Datar Vitae. Why should we hinder their process?", asked Kiara.

"Especially because the military and scientists are looking at it. The light-emitting rock was the gift of Datar Vitae to us all, to all its believers, for passing the test. Otherwise, why would it decelerate and manoeuvre right in front of us?", asked Ashok.

"These scientists, they constantly question our faith. They tell us what to believe in and judge us if we don't believe in their findings. They say the universe is made of tiny particles that we cannot see, and we are supposed to believe. If we don't, we are considered naive. But when we say that the universe was made by God, they judge us. If, and only if things go our way, they correct their hypothesis of how they understood the universe", Ashok continued.

"Tell me Kiara, what would a scientist find if he ever closely examined a shivling?", asked Ashok.

"I don't know dad."

"Nothing. It is because the texture of the power of a shivling cannot be fathomed by science. Power does not come from the rock, but by the collective faith of the people on the rock! We do not want any scientist to come and claim that a shivling does not have any power, because that scientist lacks the understanding of that power itself. *Belief can transform things*", said Ashok, as he got up, gestured towards and crowd, and started walking again.

CHAPTER THIRTY

THE LUSTROUS BOX

Covered in a hazmat suit, with scientists ogling at him from every direction, Vayu started progressing towards the box. As he stepped in closer, he tried to identify its structure from every angle. It was plain and smoother than anything he had ever touched.

"The shape, it's not exactly a cube", said Vayu from inside the test chamber.

"It looks like a cube from every angle Vayu", responded Mallory from outside.

"When you hold it, it feels - it feels like a tesseract", said Vayu stammering.

"A four-dimensional cube cannot stably exist in our hands. You understand that right?", said Vega with utter disbelief on his face.

"Maybe it is God's way of letting us perceive him!", said a voice from behind.

As Mallory ran and hugged the source of the voice, the entire room filled with scientists started murmuring.

"We need to talk Ankur. There is so much I want to tell you", said Mallory.

"There is no place for a love story on a planet that is getting blown up, Mal", said Ankur as he shrugged Mallory off and proceeded towards the centre.

"The structure is playing games with your mind, Vayu. Do you know what Macropsia is?", asked Ankur.

"No", Vayu responded.

"It is when you perceive things to be larger than they are. Take off your gloves, and feel the texture with your hands", said Ankur, as the entire crowd started getting agitated with the suggestion.

"That is a terrible suggestion, what if his skin cannot handle it?", said a person from behind.

"This has clearly been sent by someone. We all call it by different names based on our beliefs. But if it has sent something to us, that thing must have been adjusted for us to handle", said Ankur.

"Someone is out there, and it wants us to know the truth", said Vayu as he took off his gloves and helmet.

As Vayu progressed to touch the box, he felt as if his fingers were holding something much softer and lighter than what his eyes were perceiving. What looked like a lustrous steel box, on touching, felt like foam.

"It feels like it has some room to identify the object that is touching it. Like it is analyzing my fingers", said Vayu.

As he slowly turned the box and peeked into it, he saw himself. He saw himself in the clearest projection that he had ever seen in his entire life. The image of his face, that had formed on the lustrous box, was clearer than any image that he had ever seen.

"I don't know what this is, but it is clearly not from our world", said Vayu as he put down the box.

As the scientists inside the military base were examining the gift of God, it's true followers were getting concentrated on the west gate of the military base, ready to take back the blessings of Datar Vitae.

"The mob outside is growing every minute, Uncle. I don't how long we will be able to contain them outside.", said Rashid on the phone.

"You are in a freaking military base, Rashid. Contain them with whatever means necessary. I need to give some answer to the PM in the next hour!".

"It is not like we can shoot our own people, Uncle. Things are getting tense here. We need to think of something else", said Rashid, as he saw the number of gathered people.

LIGHT

The military base in Pune was not accustomed to having so many guests; that too, in the form of scientists. As Mallory sat outside the barracks, looking at the sky, the repressed sound of all the believers outside the base constantly terrified her ears.

"Can't sleep?", asked a familiar voice from the back.

"The voices from outside, they echo in my ears if I try and close my eyes!", said Mallory.

"They are fainter than the voices I have in my head. Imagine living with them, all your life", he said.

"Do you think I will ever be able to rectify this?"

"The mistake? I don't think so. But we can work on rectifying our relationship!"

"I know I have been a total bitch to you Ankur, and I am really sorry. Truly. But if I can tell you the truth before I can even begin to seek your apology, I need to find a way to forgive myself first", said Mallory.

"After you told me Mal, and when I saw the comet approaching, do you know what I felt?", he asked.

"Yes. Relief. I saw it in your eyes"

"Even after I fainted, I went into a dream state. In my dream, the world was slightly more normal, I was in a hospital bed, and just had been diagnosed with stage 3 cancer. Guess what I felt when I heard about my condition?", Ankur stared into Mallory's eyes.

"Re – Rel...", Mallory's voice broke as she was trying to speak.

"Relief. I was relieved that it was all getting over, either for me or for the world", said Ankur as a tear rolled down his eye. "I do not have the energy anymore Mal; not to fight with you, not to be upset with you, not to forgive you. I am just tired"

"Can I do anything to help?", Mallory asked, trying to find her voice in an aching heart.

"Forgive yourself and save the world. You are a much better scientist than you have been a wife", said Ankur as he got up and began to leave.

"Also", he turned back, "don't forget there is also someone else you need to seek an apology from", Ankur gestured towards Vayu, who was sitting on the far side of the barracks, looking at the couple. As Ankur left, Vayu got up and started approaching Mallory.

"I cannot do this right now Vayu. I know I owe you an explanation and an apology. But please, I can't do this right now", pleaded Mallory as Vayu approached and sat beside her.

"Light!", Vayu said softly in Mallory's ears.

"What?", she looked at him confused.

"Light is the answer. It is one of the only things that is common between us and them! Science and Math!", Vayu said, as Mallory looked at him confused.

"When I felt the box in my hands, it felt as if it was absorbing a tiny part of what I was offering it, which in that instant, were my fingers", he continued.

"So instead of a lock which we can open through a key, the box speaks through absorption. That is the way it accepts code", said Mallory getting moderately excited now.

"Bingo. I also asked Rashid to get all the media footage from the landing of the comet"

"Because of the symphony of colours that appeared in the sky, just before the Morse code", Mallory interjected.

"An amalgamation of the colours that appeared. A laser of that colour must be the key", Vayu said.

"I must say Vayu Srivastava. You are a weird guy, but you have your moments!", said Mallory, impressed by Vayu.

"Do you see what this means?", asked Vayu with a huge smile on his face.

"They are testing us! Whomsoever has sent it to us, they want to check if we are even worth their time", she said.

"I don't think they would be able to digest all our drama", Vayu said jokingly.

"I am sorry if my choices have made your life more difficult Vayu"

"I never wanted kids. I did not believe the world was worthy enough to be blessed with another life. But when I met you, just for a second in the morning at the observatory, I loved the idea of having another part of you in this universe. It just, it made me happy", he said.

"You really think I am worthy enough to have another part of me!"

"No pressure Mallory; and I promise I do not want to break the little world that you and Ankur have built. But believe me, the world is a much better place in my head, with Mallory Shah in it", said Vayu as he got up and started to leave.

"You have your moments!", she said softly as she watched Vayu leave

CHAPTER THIRTY-TWO

WEST GATE

The west gate of the military facility stood as the perfect symbol of the disparity between the two worlds. On the left stood the believers; in vast quantities, chanting the name of Datar Vitae. They had all marched down to the facility, in the hope of getting back what their god had given them, entirely clueless about the nature or the purpose of that gift. On the right stood the scientists; busy with creating a machine, something that resembled a giant laser. On the crossroads of these two worlds, right on the edge of the west gate, stood Mallory and Ankur.

"Are you sure you need to go? Vayu is the one who created this mob, let him go!", said Mallory.

"You know that is not an option Mal. Sending Vayu out with these questions can hurt their belief. They believe him to be in contact with the all-powerful Datar Vitae. They would not be able to fathom that we cannot figure this out", said Ankur.

"It is a hungry crowd out there. They haven't eaten, slept, or moved anywhere in the last two days. Going out there is suicide", said a concerned Mallory.

"I am the only one here who can do this. The disbelief you have in their beliefs, the judgment that all have you carry in your eyes, is what makes them angry. I understand them. I can get answers", said Ankur as he proceeded towards the gate.

"Are you sure we did not imagine it?".

"How can we all collectively imagine the same thing, Mal?".

"I don't know. How is it that all the videos and photographs show a clear sky? They work on the basic principle of absorption and reflection of light. This anomaly is just beyond my understanding", she said.

"Whoever is out there Mal, they are testing us. We need to come together, all of us, to pass this test. This is the test of Datar Vitae", said Ankur.

"Again, with the Datar Vitae", scuffed Mallory.

"Someone is out there. One side of the wall calls them aliens, another side of the wall calls them Datar Vitae. Both sides are unable to fathom that they are talking about the same thing. The divide between us is nonsensical. We need to get rid of the wall", said Ankur as he gestured to open the gate and stepped outside.

As Ankur stepped outside, he was instantly greeted with a warm welcome. As he walked towards the temporary slum that the believers had built for themselves, a baseball bat swung behind him and launched a brunt hit on his head. For a moment, different shades of the rainbow appeared in front of his eyes, followed by an instant blackout.

Inside the gates of the military base, half a group of scientists were busy creating a giant laser, and the other half were busy reprocessing the images from the comet landing to see if they could figure out a way to get the correct colour shade.

"Have we collected every possible image from the date of the landing", asked an irritated Rashid.

"Yes. There is nothing in any of them", Vega replied, scrolling through the results of the reprocessing software. "But I think this confirms that the colour combination is the key to the box".

"What will I do of your confirmation, my friend? What is the answer? How hard can it be? Guessing a shade of a color", asked Rashid.

"That depends on the sensitivity of the instrument we measure it with, Rashid. Looking at that thing, I think it's going to be terribly difficult", said Mallory, pointing towards the box.

"You are enjoying this, aren't you?", asked Vega with a smirk on his face.

"I mean, apart from the threat of extinction and mysterious space objects, I am happy that science is again an integral part of our lives", she said.

"None of this would matter if we cannot predict the perfect shade!", said a voice from behind.

"We are working on that", said Vayu sincerely, standing amidst them.

"All these efforts are a waste. If one image does not have the night sky, none will. Also, we still don't have the ability to capture with the same precision with which we see. Even if there is an image, the process of capturing it would have deviated the shade enough for us to fail", said Uncle pulling up a chair and sitting in front of the crowd.

"What do you suggest then, Uncle?", asked Vega.

"It's simple. If our eyes are better than a camera, what part of our body is failing us to get a better result than these damned photographs!"

"Our memory", answered Vayu, as Uncle gave him a disapproving look.

"Exactly! Who amongst us, has the best memory?", he asked, as the crowd stood in silence.

"Which genius decided that the one person amongst us, who had cracked what no one could in the history of humanity, should be sent out to deal with cult out there with baseball bats?", asked Uncle with his voice slowly rising.

"But that is the plan Uncle! Ankur is out there to get answers", said Vayu.

"What answers do you think those cannibals out there would have, that all of you collectively don't?"

"Pair of eyes, Uncle. Thousands of people who had seen the sky that day are out there. Without them, even with an eidetic memory, Ankur cannot determine the perfect RGB value of the colour shade", said Mallory

CHAPTER THIRTY-THREE

MARCH

The residents of the slums of Mumbai were habitual in making the best of their living situations. This, coupled with the newfound motivation among all the old residents, was the perfect recipe for quick affordable housing. Chanting God's name, thousands of people who were now outside the military base in Pune had found the rhythm of working in this new life. At the centre of it all, was the girl with small binoculars around her neck.

"Who is an old grandpa, who has been moving around all day, and has also forgotten to take his sweet arthritis pills?", asked Kiara with sarcasm as she handed the old man his tablets.

"You cannot boss me around now. New slum, new rules", said old Chuck popping his pills.

"Please Grandpa, I have so many things to look after. Just ensure that you pop these bad boys from time to time", said Kiara.

"KIARA! KIARA!", entered a man, shouting.

"What happened? Did Aunt Anuradha fall again?"

"The gate. They had opened the west gate", said the man.

"Are they letting us greet the lords gift?", said the old Chuck from behind.

"Hold your horses, old man. They have helicopters for everything, why open the gate?", she enquired.

"Someone stepped outside the gate"

"WHO?"

"No idea. But Salud knocked him out"

After shades of rainbow and a blackout, Ankur was finally regaining his consciousness. As he opened his eyes, he saw an old friend sitting in front of him, in an all-new avatar.

"You see Salud there? He wanted to hang your body so high that anybody who looks over the west gate sees your corpse in the sky. Bakshi there, wanted to simply burn you alive. He argued that your screams would be enough for the cowards inside to realize what would happen to them if they don't give back what is rightfully ours. Honestly, you are only alive because we could not decide!", said Kiara, lifting Ankur's chin with her baseball bat.

"Don't you remember me Kiara, we spoke about the test of Datar Vitae, the day you were reading the book. I told you the location of the object for god's sake. Why are you knocking me out?", asked Ankur, frightened yet relieved to see that she was in charge.

"I remember you Ankur, but I don't recognize you. How could you let them rob us of what we gained from Datar Vitae, that too with so much hardship? I really thought you were on our side", Kiara said as she got up from her chair.

"There is no side, Kiara, we all want the same thing!"

"Is that why you have the beaming comet locked up in there, with all your lab coats tinkering on it with their atheist hands", said Kiara as the crowd was fitting with rage.

"There is a lustrous box inside, and we think that the key to that box, is a perfect spectrum of light!", said Ankur, as he saw the crowd gasp their breath around him.

"The rock was just an outer coating, maybe a packaging to allow the box to travel in space. Inside, there is a lustrous box, something that we cannot even touch properly with our hands. We need to understand the shade of the light in the sky that appeared on the day of the landing. Only if we recognize that precise shade, will we be blessed with the blessings of Datar Vitae", said Ankur in an inspiring tone.

"What if you throw light on the box, and it upsets Datar Vitae? What if it destroys everything?", asked Salud angrily.

"Why should we believe you and your lab coats? Just hand over the box to us, nobody understands their lord more than its followers", said Bakshi.

"One man does! That man, is inside the facility, taking instructions from Datar Vitae as we speak", said Ankur.

"Did Master Vayu say something? Did he specifically ask us to remember the shade?", said an old man in a robe in the corner.

"Yes, Askok! The lord is testing us with every step. We need your cooperation", said Ankur as he looked around him.

"Very convenient of you to request cooperation now Ankur. You need our help, so you come out here and tell us that this is what Datar Vitae wants. When will you idiots stop getting confused between a believer and a fool?", said Kiara.

"I don't think any of you is a fool, Kiara. I believe in Datar Vitae as much as you do, and you know that. I am just trying to balance both worlds. We cannot segregate ourselves at this point", pleaded Ankur.

"Your ego is not allowing you to digest the fact that we don't need you. Neither do we need you to mediate our conflict, nor to explain to us how to use our lord's gift", said Kiara, as she stepped out of the hall.

"I think we can all use a break! We also have a lot of errands to complete. Let us reconvene in the night", said Ashok as he approached Ankur.

"You see that green house at the end of this road. Go! Someone is waiting to meet you", Ashok said, as he left the premise as well

CHAPTER THIRTY-FOUR

ADAPT

The aromatic fragrance of the food on the stove had filled the surroundings of the green house, highlighting the path for Ankur. As soon as Ankur entered the vicinity of the fragrance, the green house had transformed into a green home.

"Come, Ankur, step inside", said the old lady at the gate, as Ankur quickly ran and leapt in joy to hug her.

"How are you?", asked Ankur frantically

"Without a head injury. So, I would say I am in better shape than you are", she said jokingly.

"You know my injury becomes my superpower when you are there. Now that I have you and your hand-cooked food, we are going to save the world together, Aunt Anuradha", said Ankur, hugging her tightly.

"How is Mallory? Haven't spoken to her in such a long time"

"Eh! Can we talk about someone else?"

"I sense tension in married life. No drama is required for me kiddo! We can talk about whoever you want"

"She is pregnant", said Ankur with a smirk.

"THAT - THAT IS GREAT! Why are you not thrilled?", asked Anuradha as she jumped out of excitement.

"With someone else's child. She is pregnant with someone else's child"

A deep silence filled the room, as Anuradha slid back to the far end of the couch.

"Oh. Well, at least you passed the fertility test. Can we celebrate for that?", asked Anuradha.

Ankur looked at her in disbelief, stared into her eyes, giggled a small laugh and then hugged her again.

"I don't know how to feel Auntie. It aches so much, but I feel that the longer I let it ache, the further I will be from the life that I had imagined for myself", said a sobbing Ankur.

"Is that such a bad thing? Going away from the life that you wanted before?"

Ankur took a moment to consider. "If I tell you the truth, it's the worst thing in the world".

"If you know that, and you know what life you want, you will have to find it inside you to forgive her Ankur", said Aunt Anuradha as he sat next to her on the couch and she started pressing his head with a cold packet of corn.

"I cannot stop imagining what could have been, Auntie"

"Then start imagining what it can be going forward. You will find it within you to give her another chance!", she said as she put the packet down and started applying an ointment on his injured head.

"How could she? She literally ruined everything! I can't stop hating her"

"But you don't hate her Ankur! That is the whole point. Either hate her and walk away; or love her, go back, and make things work!", she said as she slowly rested Ankur's head on a pillow.

"I feel like whatever I decide, I will lose! If I go back, she will still get the life she wanted. She wins but I lose. If

I walk away, we both lose. How do I win?", he said slowly dissipating into the couch.

"You win by changing your thought process, not your decision. You are so tempted to punish her for her wrongdoings, that you are not realizing that you are punishing yourself along the way! Learn to adapt Ankur, learn to truly forgive.", said Anuradha as she started getting up.

"Where are you going?"

"To get started on a soup. Bring the corn into the kitchen when you come in!", she instructed as she entered the kitchen.

"I might not come in. I can lay on the couch and rest as well", he shouted from outside.

"You underestimate how well people know you and can predict your actions. Don't fight it, come inside and bring me the corn!", she said.

"So, are you suggesting I am too easy to read? That I should not follow my instincts and do what people don't expect from me?", he said, as he handed her the corn.

"That would be imitation, not adaptation. Don't do something because that is the right thing to do. Don't do it because it is what is expected from you. Do things that you truly want! I have known you all your life, Ankur. Stop imitating that you are the perfect husband or the perfect kid. Do what you truly feel is correct. *When you imitate, people see through you; when you adapt, you see through people*", said Anuradha as Ankur stood there in silence.

"When you go out there tomorrow, Ankur, everybody will know that you have come here to ask something from them. Don't imitate the collective voice of everybody on the other side of that gate; speak what you truly believe, and people will follow", said Anuradha.

CHAPTER THIRTY-FIVE

MESSIAH

Every soul in the slum had travelled to its centre, where Kiara and Ashok stood in the middle, waiting to hear what Ankur had to offer. Ankur, as soon as he entered, knew he had a tough task ahead of him.

"Why do we believe in Datar Vitae?", Ankur asked as he sat in the middle of the crowd, that was ogling at him for answers.

"Something only a non-believer would ask", said Salud as the crowd roared in his support.

"Did not ask for your opinion big man. Instead of being cheeky, you tell me. Why do you believe in Datar Vitae?", asked Ankur, as the crowd fell silent.

"He is the almighty who controls the stars", answered Salud, trying to get the crowd roaring again.

"You still did not answer my question. Why do YOU believe in Datar Vitae", asked Ankur again, emphasizing.

"Because Datar Vitae is the only one who can save us!", answered Salud.

"Why do you need to be saved?"

"Look around you entitled piece of shit! The way these people are living, this is not life! Your lab coats don't understand the struggle of people, how do you fathom understanding our belief?", asked an angry Salud.

"You do not believe in Datar Vitae because you think he is a god. The god that we believed in, was a supreme being, the creator, who could not do anything wrong!", said Ankur as he saw Salud boiling with anger.

"You are standing in middle of a crowd and questioning our belief in our lord. I must say, you have courage young man", said Ashok.

"Not much difference between courage and stupidity master. We don't need your lecture, Ankur. Tell us if you can help us or not. I am in no mood to waste another bowl of food on you!", said Kiara as she got up and moved towards Ankur.

"I disagree. I think you do need a lecture. I am not questioning your belief, Kiara. I am questioning your understanding of it. There is a difference!", said Ankur.

"Belief has no understanding young man", shouted Salud.

"It does if you stop and think about it. You do not believe Datar Vitae is a god because he is your creator. Nor do you believe Vayu is omniscient. How can a god, and a godman exist, who does not think about his followers, or even talk to them? You believe in Datar Vitae because you see him as a messiah who can save you", said Ankur, as he approached Salud in confidence.

"God is not only the creator Ankur, but he is also the saviour", said Kiara from behind.

"Your belief in a saviour is your coping mechanism to this failing civilization Kiara. That is why all of you, and lakhs of people across the world, united so quickly over a book by a stranger", said Ankur going and taking a seat amongst the masses.

"When you live like this, a coping mechanism is all that you have!", she said.

"I am not questioning it. In a way, *science and religion exactly provide the same coping mechanism to a failing civilization.* They both require constant faith in something that we cannot grasp completely and require us to believe that it is the answer to our misery. The problem with science is that it aims to be precise, and precision has no reverence in matters of faith. For too long, science has tried to explain itself with certainty and proof and has been humble enough to recognize when it cannot grasp something entirely. Religion, on the other hand, bases itself on the concept of a messiah. The messiah, who even if we don't understand completely, will understand things for us and bring us out of our misery. It is easier to believe that a superpower, strong beyond our comprehension is coming to save us; than to accept, that a bunch of nerds who were bullied through high school are our saviours. *It is easier to base our faith on someone we do not understand than someone who is amongst us*", said Ankur as the crowd fell silent with his words.

"Do you think Datar Vitae is coming to save us?", asked Salud as he approached Ankur.

"Yes. But the lab coats whom you all despise, we need them to unlock the gates from which the lord comes in. They need cooperation", said Ankur.

"How can they lock us out and expect cooperation? How can they hide behind the gate and expect us to reveal ourselves?", asked Kiara.

"We cannot be petty Kiara. We need them to unlock our lord's gift and help him find his way to us. We will help you, with whatever you need Ankur", said Ashok.

"But Dad!"

"Master. You will refer to me as master, and my word is final", said Ashok in a stern voice, as Kiara exited the gathering.

As the gathering dissipated to get back to their daily chores, a sobbing Kiara sat at the corner of a ledge, away from the crowd.

"Are you alright?", asked a friendly voice.

"You got what you wanted. Please give me some space", said a frustrated Kiara.

"Kiara are you fine?", he again asked persistently.

"Do you not understand what space means Ankur? Just leave me alone!", she said.

"Do you not want to help me in finding answers to the box?"

"You ask help from people who you believe are equals Ankur. What you are doing here, is just good manipulation"

"I believed in every word that I said in there. I don't speak to Datar Vitae Kiara, but I understand what believing feels like!"

"I never believed in Vayu Ankur. He who does not understand our struggles does not represent us", she said.

"Do you know my struggles?"

"Yes. Prodigy child brings his murdered family to justice; remembers specific details from his dreams. I have read the article"

"How do you know that", said a shocked Ankur.

"You have a fan who lives in that green house. All she does is yap about your achievements. If you can really remember everything, Ankur, why do you need us? You can simply try and remember the shade from that night!", asked Kiara.

"Two reasons Kiara. First, I tried, and I could not remember with precision. Second, I don't want to do it alone", said Ankur as he sat beside Kiara.

"So, you do need us?", she asked.

"Even if I figure this one out alone, what about the next challenge?"

"How do you know there is a next challenge?", she asked.

"What was the test?"

"If humanity foregoes all its differences and comes together with a promise to take better care of what it takes for granted today, the comet shall keep everyone safe whose heart is pure", she said softly.

"Even when you did not believe in Vayu, you did believe in the test he laid down, right?", said Ankur as he sat closer to Kiara.

"Exactly. We have not fulfilled the test, Ankur. The west gate that you see, that is the line of difference between us that we must forego. But it is not like we are not crossing it; it is just that you are not letting us!", she said with passion.

"I am going to ensure that we forego this difference. I am going to ensure that we all enter the facility", said Ankur.

"What! Why! You already have what you came out here to seek", said a shocked Kiara, with tears in her eyes.

"I did not come out here to manipulate or get what I wanted. I am going to get those guys to open the door, and let everyone here inside, even if it is for only a few minutes. I am going to resolve our differences, and unlock the box, all at the same time", said Ankur.

"Two birds with one stone!", she said, as she tightly hugged Ankur

CHAPTER THIRTY-SIX

SHADE

The military facility in Pune was not accustomed to visitors. While the entry of the new resident scientists was a shock to the normalcy in the facility, what was going to happen today, would be straight-up traumatic. Several soldiers, in strict formations, strode along the west gate, ensuring that the crowd from outside could enter and leave without creating chaos. Strong formations were being built, right from the entry of the west gate to the centre, so that the crowd could move along in a single line. Keeping a check on the changing dynamics, was Rashid.

"We need to create a taller stage. The stability test chamber should be visible from up there when people stand on the stage", shouted Rashid to the men who were erecting the stage.

"I don't think we should devour the walls of the stability test chamber, Rashid", said Vayu as he approached Rashid from behind.

"Uh-huh! What else do you think Vayu?", asked Rashid.

Vayu's body language changed. With his head held higher this time, he said, "I think allowing them inside is a clear mistake. This is a recipe for chaos and can jeopardize the entire operation".

"Really! You see that tree over there?", asked Rashid pointing to a tree far away.

"Yes", Vayu said diligently.

"Go tell your opinions to the tree. See if it is interested!", said Rashid as he saw Vayu's face contract is humiliation.

"I am telling you this is a mistake! You guys never take me seriously", said Vayu as he started to leave.

"You brought the god to us; how can we ask for anything more? I think we will take it from here godman", shouted Rashid, chuckling.

Outside the west gate, the people of the slum aligned themselves in a single line. As the gates opened, all they could see was that there was a long walk ahead that led to a bundle of stairs. Ankur held Kiara's hand and started to walk, with the crowd following them.

"When you said you could not figure out the colour of the sky, how is that possible? Don't you have an eidetic memory?", Kiara asked as she walked beside Ankur.

"I wish it would have been so simple Kiara. My memories, they are chaotic. I cannot remember details with precision", he answered.

"But the whole sky was painted with that colour. I don't think you should be held back by precision", she said.

"*Our memories, they are colored by emotions. The shade in which we remember images in, they are not just shades of what we see, but also of what we feel.* Do you not see the sky a little extra blue today? In tough nights, do you not see the sky gloomier?", Ankur answered.

"Is this the test then? If we want to open the box, we need to overcome what we felt in that moment, and remember the event, candidly?", Kiara asked.

"Don't you see the paradox in that statement? There is no true colour that was displayed in the sky, Kiara. The truth is the amalgamation of all our collective experiences", he said as she started walking up the stairs to the stage.

"How can the box know the truth then?", Kiara asked.

"Have you heard of the double slit experiment", said a voice standing up on the stage. On deciphering the source of the voice, Ankur quickly let go of Kiara's hand.

"I haven't", said Kiara as she looked at her.

"Light, it behaves differently when it is unobserved, than when it is interacted with. We still do not know, with certainty, the reason for this in quantum physics", said Mallory, as she extended her hand towards Kiara.

"But still, how can the box know our feelings? How can it decipher our perception", Kiara was still curious.

"Ankur here has done most of the work! He has gone back, again and again to the mental castle, to figure out the shade. But the true shade, is not his perception, but a culmination of ours. When you see Datar Vitae's gift unfold in front of you, you will feel an emotion. Just remember that night, remember the colours in the sky, and choose the shade that best represents it from this shade box in front of you", said Mallory.

"But you don't believe in Datar Vitae? How are you sure this will work?"

"I believe in your belief, and I have realized that it is all that we might need", said Mallory as the stability test chamber was unfolded in front of Kiara's eyes.

As thousands of devotees climbed up the stage to worship their lord's gift, their selections on the shade box slightly adjusted the images that were derived from Ankur's mental castle. With every person that stepped on the stage, humanity was getting one step closer to Datar Vitae

CHAPTER THIRTY-SEVEN

THE REVEAL

Everything had led to this moment. Everyone who had gathered on the marine drive for doomsday, they were all expecting the same thing; either saviour from a lord or total annihilation. Since then, what had transpired was something far beyond the expectation of any individual on the planet. From the second the sky had lit up with the colours, and the telegraphic key had communicated that it was in fact god who was trying to communicate, the journey had been dramatic and complex. After inputs from thousands of people who were gathered at the marine drive, the world was finally ready to meet the gift of Datar Vitae.

"When America was detonating the atomic bomb, they knew that there was a minute probability that the chain reaction would never stop and they would burn the entire world", said Mallory, sitting on top of giant boxes, watching the military base prepare for the big reveal.

"You think this is that moment? The moment where we can end the world", asked Vayu, sitting beside her.

"I don't know. Just because we have been gifted with something; does it mean that we should access it?", she asked.

"You think we are not ready for it?"

"Nobody gives anything for free, Vayu. In the realm of all this magic and reward that might come from the box; I think no one is focusing on the price that we might have to pay for it", said Mallory.

"If all of us together reap the benefits, it makes sense that we all pay the price, right? Look at all the people that have gathered here, the people have spoken", said Vayu, pointing to the large crowd that was helping to set up the laser near the stability chamber.

"What about this little one, Vayu? Do you think it is ready for what is about to unfold?", said Mallory, pointing towards her belly.

"It is ready for whatever its mother is ready for! Have strength for both of you, and be a little optimistic! You are going to witness a historic moment", said Vayu as he jumped from the boxes and started walking towards the stability chamber. He took a pause, turned back, stretched his hand and said, "You coming?"

Vayu and Mallory walked towards the stability chamber, where a large fencing was being created to avoid any collateral damage from opening the lustrous box. The scene at the military facility, reminisced of the doomsday. With the laser being set up, scientists were sitting with their desktops to alter the color of the laser to match the exact shade of the key. On the front, stood various military personnels along with scientists, making sure every minute thing was perfect. On the back, stood the crowd, with thousands of people shouting the name of Datar Vitae. In the far back, sitting on temporary stages, were politicians and businessmen, with the media setting up wherever they possibly could.

"Tell me honestly, what are you expecting for us to find inside the box?", asked a man in a deep voice.

"I honestly don't know. We should be prepared for anything!", said Mallory.

"We do not have time to be prepared for anything, Mallory. I am asking you a simple question. Paint a picture in your head, and tell me your worst-case scenario", he said.

"Honestly Uncle, the worst-case scenario in my head, is that the box will open with a substance that cannot exist with stability in our dimension, and the entire world will evaporate in an instant!", said a frustrated Mallory.

"Cannot get prepared for that, can we? Let us just take our chances!", said Uncle as he progressed forward and indicated Rashid to begin firing the laser.

The lustrous box sat idle in the stability chamber, around three hundred meters away from the crowd. A large state-of-the-art laser, shed the most beautiful shade of light on the box with all its intensity. As everyone sat there, holding their breath for the box to open; nothing happened.

"Why is it not working?", shouted Uncle from the front of the crowd.

"We are slightly changing the colour of the laser constantly Uncle! This could take a while", shouted Vega, standing near the computer.

The excited crowd took a heap of sigh, and eagerly waited for the magic to happen. As an hour passed by, people started to dissipate and formed small groups to chat along till the laser worked its magic.

"Big reveals aren't always how we script them in our heads, are they", said Ankur jokingly.

"Even your lord needs to be constantly engaging, otherwise the humans get bored pretty quickly!", said Mallory sarcastically.

"Everyone is here to see magic, Mal. They are not going to get impressed by a laser that changes lights!", said Ankur.

"What do you think will be in the box?"

"We will see when we get there! I am more concerned about opening the box", said Ankur.

"Makes sense", said Mallory softly.

"Let me guess, you are worried that the second we open it, the world is going to obliterate, right?", asked Ankur laughing.

"It is possible! Don't mock me for stating an obvious concern",

"You are so paranoid and cute Mal. It's uncanny for someone to be so nice and so pessimistic at the same time", said Ankur as he wrapped his arm around Mallory's shoulders.

"Compliment?", she asked.

"Obvious concern", he replied.

"Not just for me, but for this little soul in here as well", said Mallory pointing at her baby bump.

"I hope the little one carries the cuteness!"

"Not the pessimism?"

"Some of the pessimism. If it would turn out with my optimism...", Ankur suddenly stopped, and the world fell silent for Ankur.

"It will turn out with your optimism Ankur. Your optimism will get transferred to our child with his upbringing, not his genetics. I know I have robbed you of your biggest dream, but it is not all gone. Can you find acceptance for this little soul?", said Mallory as she gently placed Ankur's hand on her belly.

'I am pregnant Ankur', the voice echoed in Ankur's head. The four words he had waited for years to hear, were finally said, but with an alteration. 'I am pregnant with Vayu's child', 'I am pregnant with Vayu's child', 'I am pregnant with Vayu's child', constantly looped in Ankur's head. Suddenly, a small beam of light arose from the front, and the sky turned colourful. The exact colour appeared in front of Ankur, which had appeared on Doomsday. As Ankur turned towards the laser, he could identify the discrepancy, as clear as the day.

"Adjust the red and the yellow", shouted Ankur looking at the sky. "Make the yellow darker, red lighter, and add some more violet", Ankur constantly instructed till the laser matched the sky that was in front of him.

"You did not rob me from my child, Mal, you robbed me from my family. You were my family. When you cheated on me, you robbed me of my wife, the person I loved the most on this planet. To accept the little one, I need to first accept the person who it is growing in!", said Ankur as he removed his hand from Mallory's belly.

As the laser hit the lustrous box, the outer layer of the box started modifying itself with the colour of the laser. The entire crowd looked in anticipation, as the box was slowly turning into the shade of the laser. DATAR VITAE! DATAR VITAE! shouted the crowd as they witnessed a small crack developing in the box. As the box cracked, it rose up in the sky, cracked completely from the centre, and a small object fell from the box. The object, a gleaming disc, its surface a mirror to unseen symphonies, a puzzle waiting for the hand that holds its arcane design. As the crowd stood completely silent, in awe of the mysterious object that had been released from the box, Vega softly broke the silence!

"Is that, is that a compact disc?", asked Vega.

"What the hell is a compact disc?", asked Rashid, as the entire crowd stared at Vega in anticipation of some answers.

CHAPTER THIRTY-EIGHT

FUTURE

The military facility in Pune had completely transformed into a full-fledged manufacturing facility, with thousands of workers, working day and night in long shifts. It was exactly five months ago, that the laser had opened the lustrous box and had released the god's gift. That day, as thousands of spectators witnessed the box rising and cracking, they found a new purpose in their lives, and had resolved to not leave the facility till God's work was done. As more and more people flew in, and several nations came together to contribute resources, the slum outside the military facility turned into a bustling city. With the face of the city constantly changing, one thing remained constant: Kiara, at the centre of the masses.

"My lord, my saviour, the man who would show us the light!", said Kiara sarcastically as she entered the penthouse in the city.

"Would you stop? You know I don't care who goes in the shuttle", said Ankur.

"You might think you are smart now Ankur, but I have known you before you turned into this prick; and guess what, I can read you like an open book", said Kiara as she jumped on the couch, with her legs up the armrest.

"What does your reading say then?", asked Ankur.

"That you are exceptionally happy to be the one going!", said Kiara.

"Do you think I would have ever let that asshole Vayu go?"

"I am sure not! Anyway, it's not like you have any personal grudge against him. I am sure the decision was all professional", said Kiara with a smirk on her face.

"The way he always imagined himself to be the godman, how can you support him!", said Ankur angrily.

"I am not supporting him, boss. I am just ensuring that you don't start believing you are a godman. We really need some humans around here", said Kiara as she got up from the couch. "Anyway, your very pregnant wife was looking for you!"

"Where is she?", asked Ankur. "Scratch that, I already know", said Ankur as he began to leave.

"Remember to be a human!", shouted Kiara.

In front of the bustling city, stood the manufacturing unit. In the centre stood a dome, inside which, the lord's gift was becoming a reality. With a heavy baby bump and a cane in her hand, Mallory climbed the stairs of the manufacturing unit:

"What's the progress, Vega?", she enquired.

"We are on track Mallory. But this CD reader, it is a nightmare!", he answered.

"It is a hundred-year-old tech. Be grateful that we could source a CD reader from the technology museum. I don't think anyone alive would have even remembered how this weird thing was supposed to work!", she said.

"What kind of storage device does not allow you to copy and paste something directly, and why does the software constantly say that we need to burn the CD?", said Vayu, as he climbed up the stairs.

"It has been months Vayu, we are so close to finishing construction, and you are still fixated on the damn CD!", said a frustrated Mallory.

"I am not fixated on the CD; it's just that, why would a being so advanced, who could create the lustrous box and devise all this technology, send the details in a CD? Do they think we are so technologically challenged?", Vayu complained.

"Your ego got hurt?", said Vega sarcastically.

"Look at all this technology Vayu, if we would have gotten it in papyrus scrolls, I would have still been grateful!", said Mallory, pointing towards a large machine that was being created in the centre of the manufacturing facility.

"I shouldn't have come upstairs. You two have an old habit of tag teaming me!", said Vayu.

"We won't tag team if you go and check if part alpha is ready for operation", said Mallory.

"Will do that because it sounds like a request. Anyway, how's the little one doing?", asked Vayu pointing at Mallory's belly.

"Wondering if part alpha is ready for operation", said Mallory, bursting into laughter. Vayu gave a smirk and started descending the stairs.

"These plans are so complex Mallory, I can't imagine it has been months and I still cannot figure out the machinery", said Vega, pointing towards the screen.

"I really imagined that you would figure it out as and when we make it", said Mallory.

"When you give it a broad look, it seems like it is a spaceship, right? A vessel to take us somewhere", he said, as Mallory nodded.

"It's not. The entire force of propulsion, from what I can understand, is going towards boosting this part right here", said Vega pointing to the screen.

"Delta!", said Mallory.

"Yes. It has the most intense explanation in all the blueprint", said Vega.

"Then we just make it and figure it out as we go along. We don't have any other option!", said a voice from the back.

"What is the people's man doing up here with us simpletons", said Vega sarcastically.

"This people's man has gotten you your workforce buddy, be watchful of the sarcasm", said Mallory.

"I am sure the way they saw the CD fall from the lustrous box; everyone was on board instantly. Not much I can take credit for", said Ankur. "Did you figure out how the spaceship gets propelled?"

"No. The propulsion is only there for part delta. How would the spaceship move, no idea!", said Vega.

"What if it is a chain reaction, that propels from delta and provides a boost to alpha? Can we not figure that out?", said Mallory.

"The explanation of Delta is beyond my comprehension", said Vega.

"Show me!", said Ankur as he turned the screen towards him.

"Crafting a groundbreaking material through the lens of quantum physics involves orchestrating atomic and subatomic interactions with precision. Begin by engineering a lattice of carbon nanotubes, whose quantum confinement effects enhance conductivity and structural stability. Integrate graphene layers, leveraging their quantum mechanical properties for unparalleled strength and flexibility at atomic scales. Embed quantum dots of cadmium selenide, tuning optical properties for advanced photovoltaics and light emission. Employ quantum entanglement principles to align nanoparticles of titanium dioxide, achieving quantum coherence and enhancing efficiency in energy conversion. Coat the composite with a monolayer of boron nitride, exploiting quantum tunnelling phenomena to achieve superlative thermal insulation. This quantum-inspired recipe not only transforms the fundamental characteristics of materials but also opens vistas for futuristic applications in quantum computing, photonics, and beyond", read the screen.

"Explain it, genius", said Mallory laughing, as Ankur looked back at her in confusion.

"How are we even creating this?", he said.

"Why do you think I am looking after the construction here? Uncle and Rashid have set up a small lab where CERN used to be, to figure out how to make this", said Vega.

"Of course, we can travel in space if we figure out how this is made", said Ankur.

"There are more detailed instructions, if you are interested", said Mallory, still not able to control her laughter.

"We will worry about how to make the machine, buddy. You just worry about riding in it", said Vega, with a huge smile on his face.

"Having second thoughts, are we?", said a voice from the back.

"Not at all. Everybody out there has chosen me, I must be the right fit for the job.", said Ankur.

"You better be, cause part alpha is ready for operation", said Vayu, pointing towards the erect spaceship in front of them

CHAPTER THIRTY-NINE

DELTA

CERN, or the European Organisation for Nuclear Research, was a state-of-the-art facility, back in the early 2000s. Its particle accelerator had helped researchers unlock mysteries concerning the building blocks of our universe. But with changing times, it required two things that the people of the world no longer had the potential to give, time and money. Today, after decades of it being officially closed, it is again at the centre of a great scientific achievement.

"It cannot be done Rashid", said Dr. Muller.

"I have literally heard you say that about everything we have achieved here in the past few months, Dr. Muller", said Rashid, rushing away from him in the hallway.

"But the structural efficacy of the component itself is beyond my comprehension, beyond anyone's comprehension", said Dr Muller, chasing Rashid in the hallway.

"Do you want to explain this to Uncle? He has provided you with literally everything you could ask for", said Rashid, stopping and turning back at him.

"*Resources do not engage in science Rashid, people do. Any* amount of money is of no importance, if no one can even understand what we are creating", he said.

"But the blueprint, it is so detailed. What more could they do to help us?", Rashid said.

"They have explained to us, in parts, what we need to create. But there is no guidance on the final product. We still cannot fathom how the spaceship would look like. Sending someone on that thing, is a nightmare", said Dr. Muller.

"You leave the nightmares to us, doctor. Just make whatever the instructions ask you to make, it is that simple", said Rashid.

"The instructions require modifications at an atomic scale. With the technology that we have, the best adjustments that we can make would be to the tiniest things that one can create", said Dr. Muller.

"Tiniest things, like a needle?", asked Rashid.

"Think much smaller. Tiniest things, like a nanofiber. What would you achieve by propelling a nanofiber in space?", asked Dr. Muller.

"Aren't nanofibers a stable in industrial application", said Uncle as he entered the hallway.

"It is, Uncle. But we cannot comprehend what changing these properties would do to the nanofiber. It can be a suicide mission", said Dr. Muller.

"I will worry about that. You worry about delivering it", said Uncle.

Far away back in India, part alpha was ready for operation. With minute changes in beta and gamma, all that was awaited, was part delta from CERN. With the day of the launch nearing, Ankur sat alone in the manufacturing unit, staring at the spaceship that would decide his destiny.

The futuristic spaceship, boasted with a cutting-edge design featuring transparent windows wrapped around its aerodynamic frame. Inside the spaceship, absent of conventional consoles or control panels, laid a single ergonomic seat that rested at the centre. The pilot's role was redefined as an observer. Advanced algorithms managed navigation, environmental controls, and mission protocols, enabling the craft to independently embark on interstellar journeys while the pilot remained a passive observer, witnessing the marvels of the universe through the panoramic views.

"She is a marvel, isn't she?", said Vayu, as he entered and sat beside him.

"I am really not in a mood of banter, Vayu", said Ankur.

"Me neither. I have accepted that people have chosen you. We are beyond that", he said, handing him a beer.

"Seriously. You know I can't have alcohol before the mission", said Ankur, pushing away the bottle.

"These scientists, they only account for the physical well-being. What about mental peace? Take it, its liquid courage", said Vayu as he extended the bottle again.

"It is a medicine, that I have to agree", said Ankur as he cheered with Vayu and took a big sip. "You know I don't have any personal grudge against you, right?", Ankur said taking another sip.

"I know Ankur. It's not like I knocked up your wife", said Vayu with a small chuckle. A silence filled the room, followed by Ankur laughing.

"Phew! I thought it was still too early to joke on this. If I would had waited a few months, your child would have laughed at my joke", said Vayu chuckling and taking a sip of the beer.

"Not exactly my child", corrected Ankur.

"I am happy with being the goofy uncle, Ankur. If you can accept it", said Vayu, with a sombre voice.

"Really?"

"That is what Mallory wants. I just want to be a part of its life. In what role, I am happy to completely leave it to you guys", Vayu said, gulping down the entire beer.

"You really like her, don't you?", asked Ankur.

"She likes you, Ankur. That is what matters", said Vayu, opening a new beer.

"Any reason for this sudden pep talk?", Ankur asked.

"Just wanted to ensure that you were doing this for the right reasons", said Vayu.

"I don't think there can be any wrong reasons for doing this, Vayu. To become humanity's beacon of light, why would anybody refuse?", asked Ankur, gulping down his beer.

"I am afraid that everyone out there has been so busy making you their beacon, they have forgotten that you are also a human. A human, who is travelling to meet God. I hope you realise the risk", said Vayu in a concerned tone.

"Of course, I understand the risks, Vayu. I am not an idiot. I know I am going be the first man to ever make this space travel, that too with technology that we don't understand", said Ankur, gulping down his beer.

"Not just the journey, my friend. Even after you reach your destination. There is no Datar Vitae coming to check our intentions; but for our sake, I would need you to adjudge theirs", said Vayu in a serious voice.

"Would we be in a capacity to take any action? What happens if their intentions are impure? How do we fight them?", asked Ankur.

"I will figure that out. I have asked Dr Muller to create something for us, a side hustle. Just promise me, you will not get awestruck by your lord, and keep a practical mind", said Vayu.

"Now I feel like I should have let you win", said Ankur, with a small chuckle.

"It was not up to you my friend, like it was not up to me. It was your destiny to be our representative, and honestly, I am happy that there would be someone out there who has an appetite for some wonder", said Vayu as he cheered Ankur again and began to get up.

"I would love for the kid to have a goofy uncle", said Ankur.

"I would love for my child to have a dad, Ankur. Ensure that you come back", said Vayu as he exited the facility

CHAPTER FORTY

LAUNCH

Part delta was almost ready, and the team was gearing up for the big launch. The people of the bustling city were gathered at its centre to bid adieu to their chosen one. Around five months back, when the CD fell from the lustrous box, the big reveal had become a bit anti-climactic. With all the awe that the box had created, no one had expected a hundred-year-old tech to land in their hands. But what the gift failed to deliver with its packaging, it delivered with its contents. As soon as the CD was run, the first part of the blueprint showcased a spaceship, a docket with a seat for an individual. That day, amidst all the science and religion, politics took a centre seat to find the lucky human who would sit on that seat.

"DATAR VITAE! DATAR VITAE!", chanted the crowd as they gathered in the city centre. While the delivery of the plans had convinced one section of the society that they had encountered aliens, who in all their might, are extending a helping hand by providing technological growth; for the other section, the beaming comet had resolved for the public that it is by their prayers and resolve that their creator has arranged to meet them. While one section was searching for advancement, the other was in search of *moksha*. In the amalgamation of these two distinct paradigms, stood Ankur, through his relations on both sides of the west gate, to be the chosen one. With thousands of people chanting underneath him, Ankur stood off the stage, trying to gather the courage to climb up and greet them.

"Nervous?", asked Mallory, progressing towards Ankur.

"This is exactly what I did not want, Mal. When did I become the centre of this?", asked Ankur.

"You were always at the centre of it my love. Your obliviousness to the power that you possess, makes you the perfect candidate to wield it", said Mallory as she came and sat beside him.

"Are you not afraid for me?", he asked, almost offended.

"My intestines are screeching for me to stop you from going. But this idiot, it knows that you are the only one who can pull this off!", said Mallory, pointing at her head.

"What if I don't come back, Mal?"

"What if you bring us into a new world, where all of us have a chance at survival", she said, holding his hand.

"But the probabilities", said Ankur as Mallory put her fingers on his lips.

"I am not going to tell you that you need a bit of faith, Ankur. I know you already have that", said Mallory.

"But I don't believe in Datar Vitae", he stated.

"I know your belief is not in a creature Vayu fabricated in his head. Your faith my love, it is derived from people. It is progressed by the collective prayers of everyone standing out there, who have chosen you to lead them into the new world. I know you will come back, and when you do, we both will be here, waiting for you. The life that you wanted for us, is just a spaceship ride away", said Mallory, putting his hand on her belly.

"Love birds! We have a business to tend to. People are waiting downstairs", said Kiara as she entered the room.

"I am in no mood for a speech Kiara. I cannot address everyone out there", he said.

"They don't need your words, Ankur; they only need your presence. Let's go", said Kiara extending her hand.

"Uncle and Rashid are already on their way with part delta. Once they arrive, we need to start the launching sequence", informed Vega as he stepped in as well.

As they all went up on the stage, the crowd cheered in all their capacity. The Octacopter, with Uncle and Rashid, landed on the stage, as Vega took the mic in his hands.

"I present to you, the final part, PART DELTA", Vega shouted on the mic.

As Rashid pulled out the container with the nanofiber, the crowd truly could not see a thing; but they still screeched in their utmost capacity.

"*Give science a pinch of belief and wonder, and you get magic*", said Uncle as he saw the crowd react to part Delta.

"Where is Vayu?", asked Ankur.

"He is down there with the crowd. He refused to come up", said Vega, slowly taking the container back to the Octacopter.

The spaceship was ready, and the big day had finally arrived. Everyone boarded the octacopter to reach the manufacturing facility. The crowd stood in the city, waiting for the rocket to go up in the sky. Ankur sat idle in the seat at the centre of part alpha.

"There are no controls or consoles, Mal!", said a frightened Ankur, holding Mallory's hand.

"We couldn't figure out how this works, Ankur. You are sure, right? You can still back out, no one will judge", she said, with tears forming in her eyes.

"Do you see these? I am going out there to find out more than six probabilities", he said, touching her charm bracelet with his hand.

"But you never believed in any of that", said Mallory.

"I would constantly lecture you on faith, but somewhere down the line, I forgot the power of wonder. Science is your faith Mal, and out there, that is what is going to protect me", he said slowly sliding his hand away from Mallory's hand and putting it on her belly. "You have fulfilled my dream, let me go out there and fulfil yours", said Ankur, as he kissed Mallory's belly and leaned back to put on his seat belt. As the crying Mallory stepped back, and the spaceship pod initiated closing, a rushed voice gestured for Vega to stop closing the pod.

"Did you forget about my side hustle?", asked Vayu as he came running towards the spaceship.

"Of course not. I knew you would not let me fly in peace", said Ankur with a smirk.

Vayu slowly reached into his pocket and pulled out a small diamond, covered in a clay-like fluid.

"Are you proposing to me, Vayu!", said Ankur.

"Haha!", Vayu laughed sarcastically. "This diamond is in a superposition, Ankur. It has been quantum entangled with another one, currently placed at CERN. This is how we communicate with you when you are out there", said Vayu.

"But the second you try and take out the information, won't the entanglement break?", asked Ankur.

"We have one shot. Dr Muller has placed the other in a stable state back at CERN. Exactly after twenty-four hours, we will retrieve the information", said Vayu as he handed Ankur the diamond.

"What do I communicate?", asked Ankur.

"The harder the diamond vibrates, the bigger the danger we are in", said Vayu, as he took a step back from the spaceship.

"If all the love birds are done, can we proceed?", shouted Vega.

As the gates of the spaceship closed, everyone at the facility gulped in nervousness.

"What do you think is going to happen?", asked Kiara at the launch station.

"We are about to find out", said Vega as he pressed the switch in the control room.

The spaceship unfurled and propelled a nanofiber from its bow. Its delicate weave tore through the spacetime's fabric, setting it aglow. A sudden rift birthed a swirling vortex, and a wormhole was born, engulfing the vessel silently, in the blink of a cosmic morn. The portal's fleeting embrace was invisible to the naked eye. In milliseconds, the spaceship vanished, leaving no trace of its space. The entire team stood there, astonished by the event that had transpired

CHAPTER FORTY-ONE

SPACE

The panoramic windows allowed Ankur to see everything with immense clarity. Suddenly, as Vega pressed the switch, a bright light overwhelmed him, momentarily blinding him and obscuring his surroundings. As the light faded, he witnessed a tunnel-like passage ahead, outside of which a strange, viscous liquid flew, defying his understanding. Without warning, Ankur was ejected into the cold, dark expanse of outer space, with the spaceship free-flowing into the void. For around an hour, he was floating in a dark void with no controls at his disposal. Suddenly, he saw something familiar

"Is that, is that a red dwarf??!!", he wondered to himself, looking at the red star in front of him.

"Holy shit! There are... there are three of them!!", he said in astonishment, as he kept dangling in space.

"Can you imagine? ANKUR! Are you even listening to me?", said a complaining Mallory from his memories.

"I am listening, Mal. You are telling me about all the possible habitable planets that are there in your charm bracelet", said Ankur, sitting in a coffee shop.

"What is with Mal. Can you not take my full name?", she complained.

"Sorry if it bothers you. I just thought it suited you a lot", he said with an innocent face.

"It does, but only when you say it. Feel special, I don't allow anyone else to call me that", she said with a contained smile.

"I am feeling special. Getting to know weird names of planets that are never going to be of any use to me", he said with a grin.

"I won't tell you then. But remember, if you ever find yourself floating into space, and you see three red dwarfs and an earth-like planet, you will be ashamed that you don't know the name", she said laughing.

"I will take my chances to that happening", he said.

"Uh! I can't resist it. It's", Ankur's memory blanked. As he kept staring into the void, it clicked to him. "Gliese 667Cc. 22 light years away from home", he said as he found himself dwindling towards the planet.

Just as he reached close enough, he saw a sight that his eyes could not fathom. A single streak of light arose from one of the red dwarfs, the one that was closest to the planet. On the surface, a small machine was sucking down the planet's sun, with every second that passed. Another beam of light arose from a different part of the surface, directly pointing towards Ankur's ship. Before he could realize it, it was pitch-black darkness.

"What the hell happened?", shouted Mallory back at Earth, after the spaceship had disappeared.

"Was it supposed to happen this way?", asked Kiara, as she saw a bunch of confused scientists running around her.

"Can it be a wormhole!", said Vayu, wondering sitting in the corner.

"No time for conspiracy theories, Vayu", said Vega as he looked at the chaos around him.

"Nothing else can explain this! We saw a bright light, didn't we?", Vayu said.

"To create stable wormholes Vayu, that too on the surface of a planet, without engulfing anything else. Can you justify the madness in your theory", said Mallory.

"Should we just conclude that he disappeared through magic then?", said Vayu with a smirk on his face.

"That smirk! Vega, I am going to kill him", said Mallory in fury.

"Do any of you have any other explanations?", asked Uncle in a bold voice.

The group nodded in denial.

"Then we go with Vayu's understanding. What do you think lad, did it work?", asked Uncle approaching Vayu.

"It could have. It is all up to Ankur now!", Vayu said.

22 light years away, Ankur was slowly gaining back consciousness. As the darkness faded out, he saw himself on a beach. As the three stars in front him were slowly setting into a sunset, he saw a human coming towards him.

"Hello friend", a man, around eight feet tall, wearing a white robe, said to him.

"Are you... are you...", Ankur kept stammering, incapable of wording his thoughts.

"I am your friend. Do you see me as your friend?", he asked.

"Of course. Are you human?", Ankur asked.

"Yes. Just from a very distant future", the man said.

"Is this... Is this your planet?", Ankur asked.

"We have many planets my friend. We are, what you would call, a type III civilization in your Kardashev Scale", the man answered.

"Can type III civilizations not control an entire galaxy?", asked Ankur.

"Yes, my child. We control what you call as Milky Way. We not only control it, we birth it!", the man responded.

"What do you mean you have birthed the Milky Way? Did you create it?"

"Inanimate matter, Ankur. It could have laid in our universe forever. But what is the point of it all, if there is no eye to see it, no person to experience it?", the man said.

"Like us, were you born in a planet as well?"

"Stars, Ankur. Our inception is much more complex than your human mind can comprehend", the man said.

"Are you not...", Ankur started stammering as he asked the question.

"No, my child. I am not human. You cannot even comprehend my form, my texture, or my creation. We have limited time, ask your questions thoughtfully", the man responded.

"If you are not human, what are you?", Ankur asked slowly.

"I am your God, am I not? I am the creator, and I promise you, if the need arises, I will be the destroyer", the man said with a grim face, as Ankur's heartbeat began to rise.

"So you plant life on planets, and then meet them after millions of years?"

"HELP THEM!", the man corrected.

"Why leave your creation alone to prosper or die? Is that not cruel?"

"It is justified. Instead of feeling grateful that you got a chance to take the test, you feel disdain that you are being tested. Do you think your civilization deserves a chance?"

"All civilizations deserve a chance"

"That chance was given. We gave you a beautiful planet with more than adequate resources. We came to a rocky lifeless realm, saw its beauty, and gave its oceans the first tinker to slowly develop and become capable of experiencing it all. We gave you consciousness!"

"Is this... is this how it is always meant to happen?", asked Ankur.

"Yes. Every civilization, you see, needs to pass an inflection point. A point, that it cannot cross on its own. But for that to become possible, the civilisation needs to pass a test", the man said, slowly putting his giant hands on Ankur's shoulders.

"Did we pass the test?", he asked, with his eyes slowly watering.

"Of course. You are here, aren't you? Your world is officially saved Ankur, and you are the SAVIOUR!", the man said.

"Why did you... why did you send us the data in a CD drive? How did you know what test to give us? How did I travel so far in an instant? How are we planning to save Earth?...", Ankur kept asking, becoming a little agitated.

"Relax my child! I know you have a lot of questions. I am here to answer all of them. For now, please sit, let us enjoy the beautiful sunset", said the man as he took a seat on the beach.

"Three stars, that is a sight I will remember. One last question. Why Gliese?", asked Ankur as he sat down on the beach.

"You will know soon enough my child", the man said.

CHAPTER FORTY-TWO

DIAMONDS

"I have so many questions, friend!", Ankur said, sitting on the beach.

"I expected that. Tell me what you understand, and I will guide you through your inconsistencies", the man in the white robe said.

"You had sent the two comets?"

"Yes. The Beaming Comet as a delivery for you, and the other, the carrier of the delivery", he answered patiently.

"Oumuamua is your spaceship?!", Ankur asked in awe.

"A four-hundred-meter-long interstellar object. It was surprising you earthlings missed that one", the man said, folding his arms behind his back, and further leaning into the chair.

"Without proof, these things are called conspiracy theories on Earth", Ankur said.

"How can a species, who understands so little about the universe, ask proof for everything they cannot explain?!", the man wondered.

"Without that qualifier, humans can be manipulated to believe in anything", Ankur answered.

"That I can comprehend", the man answered with a strange smirk. A silence filled the beach for a second.

"Anyway, after realising that the comet was actually a gift from an advanced species, we opened it using the exact same colours that had appeared in the sky when it had landed", Ankur continued, breaking the silence.

"That would have been easy, right? We literally gave you the key with the lock", the man said with a continued smirk.

"I mean it took us a while, to get the exact shade", Ankur said, a bit ashamed of what he was considering as their achievement.

"A while? Do all the people in your planet still not have a perfect memory?", the man asked confused.

"No. We are really close though. Also, why the CD?", said Ankur embarrassed.

"It's simple Ankur. Your planet, its twenty-two light years away from us. That means, it takes light, twenty-two years to travel to our destination. So, when we look at your planet...",

"You see twenty-two years in the past", Ankur completed the man's sentence.

"Exactly. Due to the finite speed of light, we find it very difficult to keep an eye on a galaxy. Hence, we have created surveying spaceships that move across the galaxy, giving us an update every century. Now, do you remember if you had ever spotted the Oumuamua before?", he asked.

"Yes. In 2017", Ankur said.

"Bingo. So, the information that we have about your planet, to say the least, is archaic. Out of all your storage options at that point in time, we liked CD the best. But I understand, you guys must have moved way past that at this point", the man said.

"We have", said Ankur softly.

"Tell me more about your world. I see that you have a perfect memory!", the man said.

"I have barely cracked it myself to tell you the truth. I honestly think that forgetting is a gift for mankind", Ankur said.

"The way I am seeing your world, I don't find anything worthy to remember", the man said.

"Seeing?", asked Ankur as he got a little anxious.

Suddenly, a huge thunderbolt appeared in the sky, and Ankur instantly heard its roar in his ears.

"Calm, my earthling friend. I need you to stay calm", said the man, again putting his hands on Ankur's shoulders.

As Ankur took a few deep breaths, he saw the sky get clear in front of his eyes.

"Don't get awestruck by your lord. Keep a practical mind, and check their intentions", Vayu's voice echoed in Ankur's head.

"Does our mood control the weather here?", asked Ankur as he stared at the sky.

"Nothing like that my friend. But haven't you noticed, that when you are exceptionally happy, the sunshine feels a bit brighter", the man said, seemingly nervous for the first time.

"That I haven't, friend. But I noticed that I saw and heard the thunderstorm instantly; and where I am from, the laws of physics say that light travels faster than sound", said Ankur, agitated.

A sudden silence filled the beach, as Ankur sat alone on the beach with the stranger.

"This the idiot identifies!!", said the man, with a complete change in his demeanour, disappointed at Ankur. "He did not notice that most of the things I have been saying, I should not have known without him explicitly telling me; but he realises that we did not adjust for the thunderstorm and lightning", said the man as he got up from the beach.

"What do you mean?", Ankur looked at the man confused.

"There is a huge difference between understanding language and understanding context, you feeble man. Your civilization is not saved, Ankur. It's doomed!", he said.

Ankur stood there, silently.

"Yes, I can understand what you are thinking, without having you to open your little mouth", he shouted again, as the weather on the beach worsened.

"Around two hundred years ago, your species had landed on your own moon. We sent out Oumuamua, hoping that by when it reaches you, you will have become an interplanetary species. But no. Your imbecile wars over your ego, your distinction between your own kind, and your feeble attempts to overclaim ownership over resources only worsened...", the man continued.

"But there are a lot of qual...", Ankur began to speak.

"There are no qualities worth saving. I said I don't need you to speak to understand you", the man's temper worsened. "Do you know how rigorously we must plan these things? How many resources do we end up wasting on you? We have given you life, that is not your great filter. The filter is to survive, to develop", the man said.

"That we could not", said an ashamed Ankur.

"Yes. The more I learn about your world, the worse it sounds to me. We have been doing a recon over your world nearly every century, and the last one for humanity, was the final straw", the man said.

"Learning about it. Present continuous tense. You are in my brain, that is how you are extracting data. What do you plan to do with it?", Ankur said, shakingly with fright as it began to rain heavily at the beach.

"The genius finally figured it out! He is still asking what we will do with the people of his planet", said the man laughing maniacally. Slowly, he came really close to Ankur, and said, "I am the creator, and the DESTROYER, my child", said the man with a dead serious expression, as he turned back and started walking.

Ankur looked around him and checked his pocket for the diamond Vayu had given him. In his mind, his pockets were empty.

"If there is someone who can do this, it is you Ankur", Mallory said, standing at the beach in front of him.

"None of this is real. But I can make it real", said Ankur, as he started imagining the Rajaji palace with the white walls. Slowly, the rough weather of the beach settled down, and he saw his childhood home in front of him. As he entered inside, he saw a caricature of him, sitting in the middle of the palace, cramped up, like in a spaceship pod. Ankur slowly placed himself at its place and checked its pockets. As he gnawed through the outer covering of the diamond, he thought about his child and Mallory, and shook the diamond with all the intensity that he could gather

CHAPTER FORTY-THREE

DISAPPEARED

After hours of toiling, months of hard work and years of hoping, the disappearance of the messiah was heartbreaking for the people of the world, and especially for the believers in the military facility. Ankur had vanished with no trace, and with no way to track if he had even reached where he was supposed to. The world stood in silence, trying to decrypt the plan of Datar Vitae. Away from the manufacturing facility, CERN felt awfully quiet to Vayu.

"It has been more than twenty-three hours, Vayu. Stop this paranoia", said Mallory, as she saw Vayu staring at the diamond.

"I don't understand how the world simply does not care at this point. Why is it just a small bunch of us that are actually questioning what can happen?", he asked.

"People cared Vayu, they cared for a long time. They just don't want too anymore. I have known Chandrakant nearly all my life. You saw how he walked away, the second we opened the box", said Mallory.

"Before moving away, when he saw the blueprint, he came to me and said it is the end of our world. His voice has been ringing in my head", said Vayu.

"We each have our own fights...".

"Do you stupid lab coats have no answer?", asked Kiara in anger as she entered the room.

"We are as worried as you are, Kiara. We really have to just sit tight and wait", said Vayu.

"This is not waiting. This is desperate yearning", said Kiara.

"Whatever it is, it is the only option we have", said Mallory.

"Are you not worried?", Kiara asked.

"You have known him for fewer months than the years I have been married to him", said Mallory with a stern voice. "He will come back before this little one comes out".

"Tell me honestly Mallory, in your head, how do you see this playing out?", asked Kiara.

"I think we will get the vessel that transports us to a new world. A clean, fresh, safe start to do things better", she said as she looked at Vayu.

"You will leave this world? Not try and save it?", asked Kiara.

"Earth has run its course, Kiara. There is no point in saving a dying tree. No matter how much you water it, it will not bear fruits again", she said.

"Why just water it? Nurture it, care for it, and it will reap you better fruits than a new tree ever could. Why is it that you people can wait for years for a new tree to grow, but not care and nurture for a dying one?", said Kiara.

"A planet, like a tree, has a life span. There is no point trying to elongate it beyond what is written for it", said Mallory.

"What if the writer is with you? What if God, who makes the rules, is on your side? Then, you can elongate the life of the planet as much as you want", said Kiara.

"Okay. Then you tell me, how do you see the end of our story playing out?", asked Mallory.

"I think our creator would come, and save our planet. Provide us with the necessary directions we need to make our life here. That is how our story will end", said Kiara.

"What if the creator arrives, and punishes you for the destruction you have caused? What if the creator obliterates everything in its wake because of our failure? Why cannot it end this way?", asked Vayu.

"Even if that happens, faith would still win", said Ashok as he entered the room.

"I don't understand how any religious discussion so smoothly slips into mass genocide", said Vayu with a disappointed smirk.

"If god punishes us for our deeds, it would also create a new world free from all the evil that we have created. You want to enter into a new world Mallory, but you do not want to absolve it from what is wrong with this one. If the same people end up getting another planet, they will end up destroying it in a similar fashion. The world is not ending because of our deeds, this is the lifecycle of our universe. *Kalyug* has to end for *satyug* to come and prosper!", said Ashok.

"*The most heartbreaking reality of our time is that science is advancing faster than our ability to gain true wisdom. Our* selfishness and ignorance are leading us down a path of self-destruction. We can't keep turning a blind eye to the damage we're causing while the world around us becomes more polluted and overcrowded. Your willingness to let everything destroy is your ignorance to take any action. It is easy to sit back and let all mighty guide you on how the world runs. It is harder to step up, and take charge of creating a new world", said Vayu, getting a bit furious.

"If it is so easy, how are you so incapable of doing it? It is harder to give the handle of your life in someone else's hand", said Ashok.

"Our incoherence to accept each other's view stems from our belief and not our knowledge. *Science is not progressing faster than society's wisdom; it just takes more pride in accepting change than religion does*", said Mallory.

"We have written ourselves in a pickle Mallory. No matter how things end, one section of the society would have to pay the price for their belief", said Vayu, as he stared at the diamond.

"No matter how much you stare at it, it will not shake Vayu. THE LORD IS OUR SAVIOUR!", said Kiara.

"Honestly, I am not sure if the entanglement would also work", said Vayu as he started exiting the room.

Kiara and Ashok both gave a hard look to Mallory.

"Oh! I should go and comfort him", she said frantically as she got up to leave.

As Kiara and Ashok both sat in the idle room with the diamond, they started witnessing certain vibrations. They both knew that their lord was coming, but whether it was the creator or the destroyer, only time would tell.

CHAPTER FORTY-FOUR

VISITORS

The people of the world had gathered again to witness a change in their night sky. What started as a frantic astronomical event a few months back, had become the utmost deciding fable in the history of humanity. Multiple sources across the world had witnessed an incoming vessel towards Earth. Datar Vitae was scheduled to arrive in the next twenty-four hours.

"We are finally going to know how all of this is going to play out. Excited?", asked Vayu.

"You are enjoying this, aren't you...", said Kiara with a grin.

"Why won't I? My ending is the darkest of all. Anything brighter, and I have hit the jackpot. *The key to happiness my friend, is low expectations*", he said.

"The key to happiness is being a psychopath. *Annihilation is the most convenient exit*", said Kiara.

While people on Earth were engaged in psychological debates, up on the spaceship, Ankur had woken up on a comfortable bed. As he looked outside, he saw a 'pale blue dot', waiting for its messiah.

He jolted up and ran around the spacecraft looking for answers. Just like the vessel he had used to get to Gliese, this one also had no controls.

"Tell me, my carbon-based ape-like friend, you understand that we are not a carbon-based life, right?", said a voice around the spacecraft.

"Are you... are you invisible?", Ankur stammered.

"At this point, this is just getting sad. Can we just enjoy our time here? Don't worry, you will witness the annihilation of your planet in front of you!", said the voice.

Ankur's heartbeat began to rise. "Are you going to blow up the Earth?", he asked petrified.

"Yes, my child. You are riding on what you humans call the death star!", the man said.

"What kind of a creator kills its own children?", Ankur asked.

"If humanity fails, and the beaming comet notices even a slight hint of greed, it shall obliterate everybody in its wake, absolving humanity from the pain of a slow extinction", aren't these words from your lord Datar Vitae, whom all of you were seeking. "I looked through your head, and as I investigated the history of your planet, all I found, was greed. I am just absolving you from the pain of a slow extinction, Ankur!", said the voice as Ankur kept looking around to check for answers.

"Every civilization has its drawbacks. If you are truly the creator, you have the moral responsibility of showing us the right path. *Just because you have given birth to a child, does not give you the right to kill him!*", said Ankur, frantically looking all around him.

"Interesting! But my child is too naïve to decide for himself, and he is already dying. Should I not free him from the pain that he is experiencing?", asked the voice.

"Can you not save him?", asked Ankur, as he saw a figure getting formed in front of his eyes.

"Will the child listen to me?", the man in front of him asked, with dead serious red eyes and a grim look.

"Is this all in my head too?", Ankur asked, confused beyond comprehension.

"The spaceship is real. I am your imagination. It was uncomfortable talking with a man frantically jumping around the vessel!", said the man.

"You are our creator! Of course, we will listen", said Ankur as he gulped looking at the red eyes of the man.

"Your prefrontal cortex has increased Ankur. Why are you lying? You know you cannot deceive me!", the man said.

"When Earthlings will get to know that you are their 'GOD', they will listen. They will aid you in taking them to a better world", said Ankur.

"Making Earth a better world involves a drastic change. Steps! which I don't think your weak life form has the ability to take", the man said.

"What if we give people an option?", asked Ankur.

"It is honestly just easier to blow everything up. I have better hopes from Gliese once their life forms evolve", said the man as he started disappearing.

"Wait!", shouted Ankur.

"This is honestly getting a bit boring. I would have advanced this process, but really did not want to crumble your cerebellum", said the voice.

"Give some people the chance to go to Gliese! They will create a better world, a world you can test faster with advanced humans on the planet. The others, who will listen, you can guide them!", said Ankur, anxious, with tears flowing from his eyes.

"Not a bad plan honestly!", said the man sitting behind Ankur. His imagination had reappeared. "Why do you humans have such strong belief that your creator will nurture and protect, and not destroy? When an entity is so powerful, why trust it with your life?", asked the man.

"Let me demonstrate. My wife is carrying my child in her womb down there. Let me imagine killing my own child, because it did not turn out the way I hoped it would", said Ankur, closing his eyes.

"The repulsion to that thought, it is the strongest that I have sensed in your brain", said the man.

"We do not destroy what we create, friend. That is what makes us human. If we do not destroy our creation, how can our creator do the same?", asked Ankur.

"Saving your offspring is a survival instinct. It is in your interest to save your species by protecting your children", the man said.

"Tell me this then, why I cannot fathom killing a child who is not even mine! As humans, why did we not kill our offspring when our world was suffering from overpopulation? Why did my parents give up their life to protect mine? You might have created the tinker of consciousness in our mind sir; but how that has evolved, and how we have protected that evolution, is to our credit. It is the sequence of events you cannot repeat, and hence, you have no right to destroy", said Ankur.

"You have twenty-four hours, form the groups that want to leave and stay", said the man as he disappeared

CHAPTER FORTY-FIVE

GOODBYE!

The space vessel landed on the Earth's surface as the entire world held its breath. While not confronted with Datar Vitae, the world rejoiced as their messiah had returned.

"I knew you could pull it off", said Mallory as she ran and hugged Ankur.

"Easy with the little one", said Vayu as he came beside her and patted Ankur.

"We saw the diamond shake, is it bad?", asked Kiara.

"I might have successfully talked Datar Vitae out of a massacre. But I don't think I should take the credit", said Ankur with a smirk on his face.

"Is that the smirk I get? My god that is annoying", said Vayu jokingly.

"So, I think Datar Vitae is going to save this world. Mallory thinks he will take us to a new world. Which is the ending that we are getting?", asked Kiara.

"For the record, we were getting the ending I had planned, but someone hindered it", said Vayu with a huge smile.

"Will our child turn out to be a psychopath like him?", said a concerned Ankur looking at Mallory.

"That is a real possibility", Vayu said with pride.

"I have actually brokered a deal, where you both will get your endings", said Ankur as he winked at Mallory and Kiara.

The world was again ready for a life-changing event. Mallory, Vega, Vayu, and Ankur, stood at an elevated stage that was created by the old people in Kiara's slum. Thousands of people stood beneath, covering the entire marine drive, constantly chanting 'DATAR VITAE'. On high-rise hotels that surrounded the lavish Nariman Point, stayed wealthy businessmen, politicians, actors, and other celebrities. The rocks of the marine drive were covered with speakers that could shake every drop in the Arabian sea, with a mic attached to the stage Ankur was standing on. Reporters stood at every nook and cranny that they could find, filming the entire thing. The entire world awaited to hear the truth from 'the real godman'.

As Ankur narrated the possibility of going to a new world, Mallory stood beside him, looking at her charm bracelet, holding her new world in between her fingers. Vayu, with tears in his eyes, had finally found his place in the world. Unknowingly, he had become the author of this world-changing event, and fulfilled his father's dream. The believers, stood amongst the crowd, trembling for an ecstatic event. Their emotions could only be understood by people, who have ever truly believed in a higher power. Closing our eyes, and realizing that God has honestly come to greet and save us, was lucid and ethereal at the same time.

Science and religion have long sought to express a shared narrative, yet their intertwining is far more intricate, reflecting the complexity of both faith and understanding. As human beings, we gather our beliefs and wisdom from various aspects of existence. While religion often feels like our most instinctive guide, the beliefs that arise from it are far more layered and subtle. Similarly, in the realms of science and reason, we find ourselves as a species on a journey, continuously unravelling the mysteries of this intricate world. Along the way, we are frequently reminded that much of what we hold as truth may be flawed or insufficient. *Ultimately, the essence of true balance lies in our individual autonomy, allowing us to navigate this complex interplay of knowledge and faith.*

As every country decided places to segregate themselves into people who were going to stay and leave, the military facility in Pune again became the centre of a historic event. As all the people aiming to leave stood in the facility, and all the believers, like always stood outside it, the world was segregated again, but this time, in harmony. On the edge of the west gate, just like before, stood Ankur.

"Both our dreams stand inside the west gate Mal, a new planet and a new family, then why do I feel like walking to the other side?", asked Ankur, with tears in his eyes.

"*Faith makes all things possible; love makes all things easy*", said Mallory.

"Love is not making this easy, Mal!"

"Your faith has made all this possible Ankur, I can make all this easy", said Mallory, as she held Ankur's hand and walked to the other side of the gate.

A space vessel travelled the sky, picking up people to transport them to Gliese. Mallory and Ankur stood outside the military facility, clenching each other's hand as tightly as they possibly could, for all the nervousness in both their bodies had been navigated to that closed fist. As Ankur looked towards his wife, and their future together, he saw her eyes, fixated on her charm bracelet.

"Mal, will you tell our child the stories of how his dad saved the world?", asked Ankur, as Mallory looked at him in confusion.

"Uncle Vayu, promise me that its goofy uncle will protect it at all costs", said Ankur, staring into Vayu's eyes.

As Mallory and Ankur locked their teary eyes, he pushed her inside the west gate and the spacecraft vanished them in an instant. The God of love had worked its magic

CHAPTER FORTY-SIX

BEGINNING

Time passed quickly on the tidally locked planet of Gliese 667Cc. It had two hemispheres, one where the sun never sat, and another, where it was always dark. In the brim of these two hemispheres, stood a golden zone, with heavenly weather to stay. Five years had quickly passed since the visitors from Earth had landed on the planet, and the Earthlings had finally made a small footing on the planet.

"Ankur. Do you have any idea with how much difficulty we grow the food here? Please come and eat", shouted Mallory from a small house they had constructed.

"Chill, Mallory. We are finishing some very important business. We will be right there", shouted Vayu.

"You are the worst company for him, Vayu", said Mallory.

"What option do you have? Vega?", said Vayu, pointing towards Vega, taking a dip in the lake near them.

"We were better off on Earth. Ankur, have left the food out, please finish it", she said, as she stepped out to soak the sun.

As the newly found city on a strange planet bustled with more and more confidence after every passing day, its residents were finally becoming more accustomed to their way of life on the new planet. The new planet had provided its residents with everything they could have hoped for. Food, water, adequate climate, and an abundance of resources.

"Mom, I am hungry", a small boy came running towards Mallory, with a smirk on his face.

"Ankur, wipe off that smirk from your face and go eat. Food is there on the table", said Mallory.

The new planet had provided its residents with everything they could have hoped for. Food, water, adequate climate, and an abundance of resources. The only thing it could not provide, was their saviour, friend, husband, and dad, back to them. The remnants of the city lived a peaceful life, but the longing of Ankur stayed in the hearts of its residents.

"Mallory! there is something you should see", shouted Vayu.

"What is it, now?", said Mallory.

"Rashid is back from his expedition. He found something".

"More rocks?", Mallory asked sarcastically.

"A little better. He found life", said Vayu.

"What!!", shouted Mallory as she rushed towards Vayu.

A small creature sat in a small cage that Rashid had created. It was a small, raccoon-sized alien with iridescent fur and glowing eyes.

"They have delicate, needle-like teeth which are perfect for gnawing for minimal sustenance, but they barely consume enough to stay alive. They have a social nature and dwell in sprawling, communal nests that shimmer faintly in the twilight. Despite their frail appearance, their colonies are intricate and resilient", said Rashid.

"Are they dangerous? Aggressive?", asked Vayu.

"Not from what we have seen. They live quite far away and are generally scared and not very smart. But they might pose a threat in the future", said Rashid,

"What do you suggest?", asked Vayu.

"We have the capability to destroy their colonies. But it would take months", said Rashid.

"NO! No killing, and no destroying colonies Rashid", said Mallory.

"We need to differentiate ourselves from the beings we were back on Earth. Don't forget", said Vayu.

"With each life we save, we save humanity", said Mallory, as she freed the little creature from his cage.

As the raccoon-sized alien ran back towards its colony, the new residents of Gliese looked at the great night sky, waiting patiently, for a new beaming comet.

Epilogue

Science and religion have long sought to express a shared narrative, yet their intertwining is far more intricate, reflecting the complexity of both faith and understanding. As a fair ending to this intricately complex narrative, it almost feels diabolical to take a side, or even allow two separate distinctions.

It is fair to assume that the reader has chosen a side here, reflecting an inclination to this solid interplay of faith and reason. But while the God of love has allowed for this fair distinction, it is naïve to believe, that the answers to these complex endeavours are ever so simple. While the characters in the story do get a choice to choose their beliefs, the entire imperative point of the narrative, is to understand that there really is no choice.

The people who have stayed back, trusting their God to lead them into a better world, might be greeted by a creature who just understands the real complexity of our universe. The path that the lord sets, would ablaze with scientific knowledge that aids humans in making better choices, only sometimes reflecting as religious dialects. What is mythology, if not the story to showcase what is right? Belief in a creator, or in a destroyer, is sometimes the ultimate driving force for people to make tough choices.

As for the people on Gliese, the hardship is not to follow the righteous moral path today, but after centuries. What if our old religious texts, that drive us to make morally righteous decisions, are just them repeating stories of the truth of a creator that they had seen? When our characters have seen an almighty power today, it is easy to motivate them to follow the correct path. But, centuries down the line, will reason be enough of a deterrent to pass the test, or will our scientists take the help of mythology?

Science and religion have long sought to express a shared narrative, yet their intertwining is far more intricate, reflecting the complexity of both faith and understanding. Only by acknowledging the true nature of this complexity, we can strike the real balance.

www.ingramcontent.com/pod-product-compliance
Lightning Source LLC
Chambersburg PA
CBHW021356150726
47989CB00005B/2271